HEALING STORMS

LYNN BURKE

One stormy night breaks Kane Austin. Moving deeper into the Pennsylvania woods doesn't heal the heartache of his tragic loss, nor does it offer the peace he longs for. He certainly can't bear the thought of loving again.

Charley Woodhill blames himself for his sister's and niece's deaths. He feels he doesn't deserve Kane's forgiveness, and especially not his love, but that doesn't keep him from watching over his best friend from afar, coveting what he can never have.

Determined to live a quiet life, Jill Walters isn't looking for a man or complications. But flames of desire bright as a lightning strike can't be denied, and the consequences of falling for not just one but two men shake her unstable foundation.

Will Kane let go of the ghosts from his past? Can Charley find the strength to share the man he's longed for since childhood? Or will Jill choose for them and flee to keep the two men safe?

CONTENTS

PROLOGUE

ALANA

A crunch of metal and my world shifted between red and black—blood and death.

Ears ringing and the scent of gasoline stinging my nose, I fought for breath as all movement ceased around me. Blinking my eyes as the numbness of mind began to fade, pain radiated from my skull and down my back, shutting off completely at my waist. I couldn't feel my toes.

Rain continued to pound against the car—I couldn't move more than the hand of my arm that pressed between my chest and metal.

"Nat?" I gasped, trying to call out to my four-year-old in the backseat since I couldn't turn to check on her. She didn't answer, and I blinked again, trying to clear the hot wetness sliding down my forehead into my eyes.

"Nat?" I tried again as headlights swept over me, the rumble of another vehicle cutting out seconds later.

"Alana!" My twin brother's scream reached me, and I tried to move, the panic in his voice making me want to get to him

—soothe him. I should have let him take us home. Should have let him...

"Alana! Oh, God. Oh, fuck … Alana." His hand cupped my cheek, and I fought to focus on his face through my shattered driver-side window.

I smiled… or I tried to as rain dripped off the end of his nose, his dirty blond hair soaked and plastered to his head.

Lightning split the sky behind him, and thunder cracked one second after the bright flash.

"Charley," I croaked on a whisper, my chest growing heavier as he wiped across my face. "Sorry. Should have let you…"

"Shh. Hold still. An ambulance is on its way."

Ambulance.

"What h-happened?" Shooting pain raced down my spine … it hurt to frown.

"You hydroplaned." He swallowed and cursed as hot wetness continued to slide down my forehead and over the bridge of my nose. "Hit a tree."

Stubborn. I'd been too damn stubborn.

"Nat?" I whispered.

Charley left my field of vision, but I couldn't turn my head to track where he'd gone.

"Oh, no. Oh God, no." His voice cracked, and I closed my eyes.

"P-please tell me she's okay, Charley," I sputtered through the wetness dribbling down over my mouth. I couldn't have hurt my baby. *Please, God.*

He came back to my window, his face pale even in the headlights of his truck illuminating the immediate vicinity.

Another flash of lightning and the grief in his eyes caught a sob in my throat.

"No," I whispered, my eyes welling. *Stupid, stupid woman.*

"Hang on, Alana." He yanked his sweatshirt off, tenderly wiped my face, and pressed the soft cotton to the side of my head.

"Charley?" Focusing on his face proved hard, and I blinked at the haze of red.

"You're going to be okay." His jaw clenched, and lightning flashed.

"Nat?"

"It's not good, Alana."

"H-help her!" My voice rose as motherly instinct grabbed hold of my heart, and my body fought to move—but couldn't. "Help my baby!"

"I can't," he choked out. Another flash lit his face, and I *knew.*

A lone whine rose in my crushed chest as the realization I'd killed my baby knifed my heart.

"Noooo!"

Charley held my gaze, his palm warm on my neck while holding his sweatshirt on the wound I realized had dripped the blood into my eyes and over my face.

"No, Charley..."

He didn't answer, and I couldn't twist from the metal crushing against me on all sides. I couldn't see my baby ... couldn't hold her.

"Charley!" I holler whispered, my lungs constricting, my heart breaking.

"I'm so fucking sorry," he whispered, his voice ragged. "Hold on for me. Please."

My gaze slipped to the darkness beyond him, the trees in the distance lighting up like noon with another flash from the storm hovering above. Deep shadows beckoned, promising to relieve my pain, my grief.

"Alana."

I gasped for breath.

Sirens wailed in the distance, but another truck rumbled close, headlights flashing. A car door slammed.

"Alana! Nat!"

Kane. I relaxed in my steel cage at the sound of my husband's voice. *Everything will be okay. He'll forgive me. He always does.*

My man, my first and only love, dropped to his knees beside Charley, his hands finding my face as my brother gave him room.

"Alana," he whispered my name like a prayer, and as with every time I stared into his hazel eyes, my lips lifted.

"I'm so sorry, Kane. I-I shouldn't have left. So … sorry."

"It's gonna be alright, love. I forgive you. We'll get you out of here, and you're coming back home. Promise." He glanced behind me as though searching for our daughter, and Charley clasped his shoulder.

"Don't, Kane," my brother mumbled, but Kane tore from his grasp and disappeared to check on our daughter, his anguished sobs a mere heartbeat later, ripping me apart.

"Oh, God. No, no, no … *Nat!*"

Tears slid down my cheeks as fists pounded on metal.

"Kane!" Charley hollered at him, but my husband continued to try to get to our little girl, fists banging on metal.

"She's dead," I whispered, but neither man seemed to hear me over the crash of thunder. *My fault.*

Darkness crept in around the edges of my vision, and I fought to stay conscious. Rain slashed at my face as the wind shifted. Thunder boomed, shaking the mangled car around me. One fight, unkind words. *I shouldn't have left.*

"We've got to get them out!" Kane hollered as my eyesight hazed.

Sirens drawing closer and flashing red and blue lights kept me conscious.

Time slowed—or did it pass at all? Cold raindrops pelted me through the broken-out windshield in slow motion, my eyelids barely moving to blink them away...

A face I knew well slid into the window, returning reality in vivid detail.

Pain.

Cold.

The soft murmurings of my brother, trying to comfort my wailing husband, reached me over the rain pounding on metal, but my focal point became life. Hanging on regardless of guilt and shame as the face in the window peered at me.

"Andy." I tried to smile at the EMT I bossed around while on duty at dispatch. Rain dripped off the long dark strands of hair hanging down over his forehead.

"Alana." Lips thinned, his dark gaze flitted over me, hand gently lifting Charley's sweatshirt from my head.

"How bad?" I managed, blinking to stave off the darkness, cold numbness creeping across my fingertips and through my heart.

He hesitated before answering, "Not good."

My chest ached, more from grief than the crush of the

wreck around me. "Nat?" I whispered as lightning flashed across the sky, the crack atop it shivering my skin.

Andy disappeared and returned before I could draw breath, shaking his head.

"Andy?" I squeaked as he refused to meet my gaze and surveyed the damage I couldn't see around me, the metal pressing against my chest.

Feeling my pulse, he finally looked me in the eye. "Kane!" he called, his voice firm. His furrowed brow and the worry in his eyes said it all. "Your wife needs you!"

I struggled for breath.

"She doesn't have much time," I barely heard Andy tell my husband, and my pulse slowed.

Clarity broke through the slashing rain, the pain in my back, and my heart. I blinked against the rain.

I'm going to die...

My life didn't flash before my eyes, simply the face of the man I had adored since we'd been children—my best friend, my twin brother's best friend, my lover.

He fought to be strong for me, but his working throat and the anguish in his beautiful hazel eyes betrayed his heart—my sweet, loving man.

"So sorry."

"Shh." He tried to smile but sobbed. "Okay, Alana. It's okay."

It wasn't.

"Kiss me," I whispered, needing his forgiveness, his love, knowing I couldn't go to the grave without it.

A gentle brush left his lips tainted red with my life's blood. I blinked hard against the blackness creeping into my periphery.

"Always love you," I whispered. "Always be with you. No more … long walks after d-dinner." I grimaced, wondering how much longer I had. "I'll b-be there in the breeze, though." I gasped for breath as he gripped my hand, squeezing tight the beads of Nat's favorite bracelet between our palms.

"Don't leave me," he begged, his voice broken and lips trembling.

"I'll whisper sweet nothings in your ear." He loved my breath on his neck and ear.

"Alana, *please.*"

I lifted my gaze to Charley behind my husband, stoic as always, another flash of lightning showing fists clenched at his side and rain slashing at his body. He would find a way to blame himself, even though I'd insisted on driving.

"He'll need you," I whispered to Kane. "I know you've always … loved him."

Pain lanced through my chest. *Oh God, the pain…*

"Alana."

"Maybe he'll—" I gasped for breath.

"Don't go, my love." Kane kissed my lips hard, his sob escaping into my mouth. "Don't go." He peppered my face with kisses, the rain dripping off his nose to mix with the blood smeared over my face as his pleadings faded in my ears.

"Please don't go. Don't leave me all alone. I can't do this without you, Alana. *Please.*"

"Charley … always love…."

Darkness won, and the weight lifted off my chest as my vision faded to black.

5 YEARS LATER

Rain pelted the roof of my cabin as I laid in my bed, eyes wide open, staring into the dark. Lightning flashed, and thunder rumbled, rattling my window and heart alike. I'd put the metal roof on purposefully, fully intending to heal my PTSD from the night that broke me down to a mere shell of a man.

Widowed.

No daughter to hold and watch as she grew.

All because of a torrential downpour and one stupid fight over something so small, I couldn't even remember what it had been about.

My throat tightened, and I pressed my fists against my eyes, cursing God, cursing the sky, every boom outside flinching the muscles beneath my skin.

Five damn years I'd suffered, and no amount of therapy had helped. I'd lost my happiness, and finding it again seemed impossible—not that I'd truly tried. Whatever words I'd spewed that night had sent Alana running—I blamed myself for what had happened.

I crawled from bed even though I didn't need to get up for work for another hour. Coffee had become my morning companion rather than the beautiful blonde I'd adored since the fifth grade. I listened to the pot brew rather than my daughter's childish laughter while she crunched on dry cereal.

My throat clenched as I shuffled out of my bedroom.

Moving out of our house and one town over, deeper into the woods of Pennsylvania, didn't bring the new beginning I'd hoped for. Didn't offer the inner peace I searched for with every breath that filled my lungs. Visiting my parents back home only brought more heartache as memories of the twins next door swarmed my brain.

Alana Woodhill, the girl I'd adored and managed to talk into marrying me.

Charley Woodhill, her older brother by all of two minutes, was my best friend and had been closer to me than my own brother.

He'd been my right hand since childhood, my best man when I'd married his sister. I felt I lost him that night, too. He'd shut down, shut me out, but I hadn't reached out to him to bridge the gap Alana's death had somehow caused between us, either. I distanced myself completely, hoping to avoid any remembrance of what I'd lost.

Pain and grief still wrapped me up in darkness. I couldn't seem to escape its claws.

I blew out a heavy breath and grabbed the container of coffee from beside the pot, flipping open the cap with shaking fingers as another boom of thunder split the sky.

Empty.

Teeth clenched, I closed my eyes and cursed. How the hell

had I forgotten coffee when I'd gone shopping the day before? With Alana gone, I struggled to remember the simple things in life. Like adding goddamn coffee to the grocery list I never wrote out and tried to keep track of in my mind.

To waste time and drown out the storm still raging overhead, I hopped in the shower. I hadn't sported morning wood in years. Hadn't gotten it up, even to the good memories of sharing a bed with my wife. Celibate, and as far from wanting a woman as could be, I enjoyed the spray of hot water without taking myself in hand and squeezing one out like I'd have done years earlier.

The storm receded enough for me to relax by the time I climbed out of the shower, red and prune-like. Needing coffee and able to handle the leftover sprinkles still falling from the sky to splatter on my truck's windshield, I got dressed for work and headed down the mountain in my old Ford.

A little mom-and-pop store sat a mile down the road, my favorite spot to grab a cup of joe whenever my tub of Folgers turned up empty. The rain stopped completely by the time I hopped out of my truck onto the pebbled parking lot and slammed the door behind me. Shoulders hunched in my flannel against the cool spring breeze and occasional spit of rain from the lightening sky, I hurried inside the wood slab building, the tinkling of the overhead bell announcing my arrival.

Annette Edwards, the co-owner of Mountain View Store, stood behind the counter, her smile like the bright sunshine, her crooked front teeth as endearing as her ruddy cheeks and the many wrinkles on her face.

"Kane, my boy!" Her watery blue eyes twinkled, and she

rounded the counter to hug me tight. "How've you been? Haven't seen you stop in here for coffee in weeks!"

Heat rose to my cheeks as the motherly-type woman held me at arm's length and checked me out.

"Trying my best, Annette."

She tsked between those teeth. "You need to take better care of yourself. Come on. I've got some chocolate chip muffins Roy baked up this morning. I'll get you one along with your coffee."

Roy Edwards was the love of her life, the man she'd been with for over sixty years, and the man who helped run their little store in the middle of nowhere.

"Speaking of Roy," she said, pulling a muffin from the small display case atop the counter, "we want to put up two more cabins out back."

"Rental business booming?" I asked, taking the muffin. Homemade baked goods—hadn't had near enough of the damn things over the last couple of years. Alana had been one hell of a cook...

"We rented every week last summer—all summer long," Annette kept me in the present, her hand steadier than mine as she poured me a to-go cup of coffee. "Figured it might be worth the investment."

"Not retiring anytime soon, I take it."

She chuckled. "Pfft ... no."

I glanced out the store's back window while making my way to the aisle holding cans of coffee, chowing down on half of the muffin in one bite. Three tiny cabins nestled against the woods, two with vehicles parked out front, but there was certainly plenty of room for more along the property's tree line.

"When can you start?" she asked as I set the Folgers down on the counter, the other half of the muffin in my mouth.

I picked up my steaming cup for my first sip of the day before replying, that feeling of *ahhh* hitting me straight through to my stomach.

"Work's picked up at the mill, but I could be here on weekends. Maybe grab a couple of guys to help me get them done quicker if you've got a deadline."

"We want to employ *you*, Kane." Annette patted my hand resting on the counter. "Put in time when you can, as you can. If it takes an extra couple of weeks, that's fine."

"I could get things rolling whenever you're ready."

Annette winked as I handed over a ten for my coffee and the muffin. "Roy already drew up the plans." She gave me my change. "Don't go anywhere. Be right back."

She shuffled through the door behind her, which led to the attached ranch home she and Roy had lived in since their thirties.

I sipped my coffee, beyond thrilled to have something to fill my weekends since I'd given up going out. I'd taken to making furniture in the woodshop I'd built alongside my house over the long hours. Everything in my cabin had been handcrafted, my loneliest days spent on cutting, whittling, and fitting wood together, the old-fashioned way.

I'd become a true craftsman, even selling things to the locals on occasion. The hobby kept my hands busy but left too much time to think.

The back door opened behind me, pulling my focus off the napkin crumpled in my hand. A woman I didn't recognize slipped into the store, her head down, her dark, silky hair a cascade clear past her shoulders. A pair of jeans clung to shapely legs, and a flannel hung open, revealing a tank top fitted tight enough to show off one hell of a rack.

I swallowed and frowned as my dick woke up from its long-ass sleep.

The hell?

Instant guilt slammed into me, and I looked away from the woman, my hand once more shaking as I lifted my coffee.

Annette returned before I could give the guilt further consideration, and although the hairs on my arms threatened to rise from the noise of someone else in the store, I didn't turn to acknowledge the woman behind me.

"Here you are." Annette handed me a pristine piece of graph paper, the layout lines dark with pencil, perfectly drawn with a ruler.

"Just like the others?" I asked about the other cabins I'd built three years prior while checking out Roy's drawing.

"Just like the others."

I pretended to study the simple plans while my ears strained for the woman behind me. Footsteps moved closer.

"Jill," Annette said, "this is our local handyman, Kane Austin. Kane, this is our new employee, Jill Walters."

Not having a choice, I turned, my fist crumpling the plans as my gaze snagged on eyes the color of a chestnut, rich and brown, fathomless—guarded.

I nodded a greeting, thankful as hell my hands were full so I wouldn't have to touch her. "New to town?"

She licked her full lower lip and glanced out the store's front picture windows while hugging herself as though she wanted to whither up and sink into the floor. "Yes."

"Jill agreed to be my new set of hands since mine are

getting knotted with arthritis," Annette said, but I couldn't look away from the pink flushing Jill's cheeks.

My dick sure as hell was interested and let me know by swelling fully inside my Carhartt work pants. Alana had been the last person I'd thought of in that way, and although shame flushed through me, my focus remained riveted on Jill's face. As though my continued stare unnerved her, she bit her lower lip and refused to look at me.

A feeling I almost didn't recognize swept through me, and I found myself wanting to pull her close and protect her from whatever had caused her to be so reserved, so nervous around strangers—or maybe men.

Brow furrowing and my stomach in knots, I turned back toward Annette. "I could probably have the foundation guys pour the slabs by Friday, so the concrete will be dry for me to get started on Saturday. Tell Roy I'll give him a call tonight."

She eyed me, the wrinkles on her forehead doubling. "Will do."

My attention strayed back to Jill unintentionally, our gazes locking for a split second, catching my breath.

Fuck.

"Nice to meet you," I forced myself to say, wanting to mean it, and she mumbled the same. Teeth clenched, I stalked outside and inhaled the cool air until my lungs hurt. I'd disrespected Alana's memory. Cursing myself up one side and down the other, I stomped toward my truck.

A nervous little bird, Jill Walters sure as hell had grabbed my attention, and I wanted to hate her for it. I'd never been anything but faithful to Alana, and I refused to disgrace myself by getting hard as hell over a mere stranger.

New to town and working for Annette and Roy Edwards,

meant she'd likely be around for a while. When Annette decided you were hers to look after, you didn't have much say in the matter.

I need to stop at the grocery store after work and pick up a couple cans of coffee. Otherwise, I might end up doing something I regret.

I tossed the crumpled paper in my hand onto the dashboard while climbing into the truck, my focus following it as it rolled to a stop in the far corner of my windshield.

Plans for the new cabins.

"Shit." Lips pursed, I slammed my door and considered calling Roy to tell him I couldn't work for him, but I wouldn't do that to the old man. He'd been nothing but kind to me when I'd moved up the mountain from their store. He'd even hooked me up with the guys who drilled my well and the electrician who had connected the wiring I'd run.

No. I owed the Edwards more than a thanks for all they'd done for me. The extra work would also keep me busy. Require more of my brain's attention, too.

I would just need to avoid the dark-haired woman, the nervous little bird who intrigued my dick and evoked the protective nature I hadn't felt in a long-ass time.

My truck rumbled to life beneath me, and I took off, my gaze on the road instead of searching through the storefront for another glimpse of Jill. More curses rose to my lips, but I clamped them shut, apologizing to Alana in my head instead.

She'd never once spoken to me on the breeze, but her promise to love me forever made me feel I owed her the same, regardless of my mom's attempts to hook me up with local singles and my dick's sudden interest in the newest girl in town.

At least work would punish my body, and I would have something to focus on for the next eight grueling hours. Maybe I would grab some lumber to keep me busy in my woodshop afterward.

I hoped nothing else would disrupt my day. Fuck knew, I'd had enough already.

JILL

*E*ight years of hell, finding the balls to run to freedom, and my body lit up for another man, even though I'd sworn off the bastards.

His lumberjack shoulders had caught my eye at the front of the store, and I made myself scarce instead of going straight to scrub the tiny public restroom. Straightening shelves behind him, I waited for Annette to return. I should have gone up there and helped him as I did with other customers whenever Annette needed a break rather than hide and sneak peeks of him.

My second glance had snagged on his backside. Round and biteable beneath tan, workingman's pants, I couldn't help but stare for a few seconds. He stood a few inches taller than my five-foot-nine, and light brown hair topped the head he kept lowered while I'd check out his backside.

Annette came through the door to their home and handed him a piece of paper. "Here you are."

"Just like the others?" His rich tenor held a sexy rasp, the type that worsened his appeal in the best way possible, damn him.

That light he'd flicked on in my body flared, heating me from head to toes—tingly, wet.

JD had always accused me of cheating on him, although I'd remained physically faithful to him. But my mind? Not so much. Fantasizing about a loving man—a *kind* man— tempted me when JD's words had torn me down. So, his accusations of being a cheating whore? Pretty much true.

I'd survived my years under his verbal and emotional abuse, reasoning it away as stemming from insecurities my love could help him overcome. He'd never healed, and I'd stayed too long, hoping for the best, as I always did.

Pushing those thoughts aside, I approached the counter, determined to live my new life from beneath his shadow like I'd been attempting to do for a handful of months.

I am beautiful.

I am independent.

I am strong.

The daily affirmations I'd been encouraged to repeat by the woman who'd helped me escape hadn't rid my mind of the negativity JD had harmed me with, but I'd definitely made progress from than the cowed woman I'd been months earlier. Those steps hadn't erased my timidity fully, but I tried to change my thinking, as she'd suggested.

Annette made introductions, and I caught a glimpse of Kane's darkly lashed hazel eyes before ripping my gaze away.

So much pain...

Can a man be hauntingly beautiful? *Yes, and why does he have to smell like soap and the outdoors, a drool enticing man?*

"New to town?" he asked.

Questions. I hated questions, and everyone in the mountains where I'd finally settled seemed full of them—Annette especially.

I licked my lower lip and glanced out the store's front, my arms winding around my center on their own as I hunched beneath my flannel to hide my pebbling nipples.

"Yes."

"Jill agreed to be my new set of hands since mine are getting knotted with arthritis," Annette said.

The feel of his stare heated my face, and I bit my lower lip. A few seconds of silence hovered, and I wanted to sink beneath the worn wooden planks under my sneakers.

Kane mumbled something else about slabs and work on Saturday.

I snuck another quick peek at his profile—strong brow and slightly crooked nose, groomed beard, and thick lips. *Definitely beautiful,* I thought with an inner sigh as tingles I didn't want to enjoy intensified.

"Will do," Annette told him.

Kane glanced at me once more, and I couldn't look away fast enough to avoid his gaze. I swore time slowed as I saw straight into the deepest parts of him.

A depth of sadness, only another shattered soul would recognize, filled his eyes. A complete stranger, yet my heart ached for him. The comfort I wished to give him outweighed the sexual need he'd brought to life in every cell of my body.

"Nice to meet you."

I managed to sputter the same, and he spun on his heel, shoulders hunched like my own. My gaze trailed after him as he walked out of the store, the bell on the door jarring me back to reality from the rabbit hole of his pain and the longing to wrap him in my arms.

Calm yourself, woman.

Blowing out a breath, I turned toward Annette, forcing a smile. She and Roy had been lifesavers, giving me the job and tiny apartment above the store, minutes after I'd asked about the *Help Wanted* sign in their window.

She eyed me with a knowing look, but no trace of a smile lifted her wrinkled lips. "Easy on the eyes, isn't he?" she asked, and I shrugged.

"I used the last of the glass cleaner yesterday," I said, ignoring her truthful statement.

"Just grab a new one off the shelf. Want a coffee?"

"Sure."

She turned away, and my mind went straight to her last customer. Kane Austin, burly lumberjack type with shoulders wide enough to carry a woman's burdens, but he seemed to struggle beneath his own.

"Kane's a widower."

I gazed at the back of Annette's hair and the thinning curls she attempted to fluff to life. "Oh?"

"Lost his wife and daughter in a car accident five years ago," Annette explained while poured my coffee.

"He's still grieving," I said, my inner focus going back to the pain in his eyes. *Poor, poor man.*

Annette turned and handed me my coffee, her lips pressed tight as she nodded. "Built himself a small cabin up the mountain behind us. Hasn't been out with anyone that Roy and I have seen. A real shame, all that man going to waste."

A heartachingly beautiful man, I didn't expect to forget

anytime soon, unfortunately.

"Guests in cabin three are checking out today?" I asked and sipped my coffee, needing to change the subject.

"By ten."

"I'll get started on the bathroom in here once I finish my coffee, then tackle the ones out back," I said of the bathrooms attached to the store for the renters since the primitive cabins didn't have running water.

"Take your time, child." Annette settled on the plastic chair she kept behind the counter, its frayed seat cushion evidence of the years she'd spent sitting on it. A stack of worn paperback novels sat on the shelf behind her. I'd found her focus deep inside one whenever a customer didn't require her attention.

She didn't reach for her book but eyed me until I shifted, ready to flit back outside and up the open stairs to hide in my apartment, but I had work to do.

"Sleep better last night?" she asked before I could turn away.

I hadn't, but I nodded and sipped again. I'd made the mistake of letting it slip, I didn't sleep well—ever—but hadn't shared the reason was nightmares of JD coming to find me. I'd offered Annette the excuse of restless leg syndrome, but that, too, kept me moving—straight up from western Maryland where we'd lived. I'm surprised I'd decided to stop and stay for a while, but the small store, the mountains surrounding it, and the sense of rightness had me wanting to settle in for a time. Add in Annette insisting on treating me like her daughter, and I didn't have much choice. My heart caved at the feeling of being needed, appreciated, and my agreement followed.

Jogging five miles every morning helped with keeping my itching feet in place, regardless of where I'd traveled the previous months, searching for an obscure place to settle down.

A truck barreled across the parking lot, its backfiring muffler and mud-slinging tires drawing both our gazes to the huge front windows with a mountain view to die for. The driver slammed the truck into park, his raised voice reaching us through the glass separating us.

I couldn't make out what he said, but his tone said it all—never mind the stooped shoulders of the woman in the passenger seat.

He screamed.

She cowered.

My nerves squeezed tight, twisting my stomach and souring the coffee I'd drank.

"Davison." Annette tsked beneath her breath while rising to her feet. She huffed a snort. "Damn man."

The guy's arms raised, his face red, his mouth going, and tears stung my eyes for the poor woman even though he didn't hit her. A second later, he hopped out and slammed the door, stalking toward the store with a dreadful scowl, sending my pulse into high gear in the worst way possible.

"Fucking worthless bitch!" Those words came clear through the door the second before he wrenched it open.

Similar words from a different voice rang in my memory. I set my coffee down and scurried toward the restroom, locking myself in and fighting to keep from giving over to a rising panic attack. Over the thumping in my ears, I could hear him and Annette talking, but I closed my eyes and bent at the waist, my hands on my knees.

Breathe.

Breathe.

Relax.

It's not JD.

I am not worthless. I am not unlovable.

Voices quieted along with my pulse, and I forced my mind to focus on the porcelain and tile I'd deep cleaned my first day on the job. God bless her arthritic hands, Annette had tried to keep the store in decent shape. She'd thanked me countless times since I'd taken over the cleaning chores.

The bell tinkled—another customer or the asshole leaving?

Heart slowed to almost normal, I listened at the door. Not hearing voices, I let myself out of my self-imposed prison, my hands still shaking like crazy. A quick glance out the front window revealed the asshole had indeed left. A heavy breath escaped me, my shoulders relaxing at seeing his truck gone, and I approached the counter to grab the coffee I'd left behind.

"Roy is putting a pot roast in the crockpot for dinner tonight," Annette said. "You're welcome to join us."

"Thanks," I whispered and grabbed my cup. "I'd like that."

She and her husband had taken me under their wing, and although they sure liked to dig, I found myself not wanting to push away their kindness and hospitality. It was nice to feel wanted for a change.

I started toward the utility closet to get the cleaning supplies.

"A good man, my Roy." Annette's words paused my feet.

"The best," I agreed.

The old man adored his wife, and any time I caught the

two of them outside together, their hands clasped as though they couldn't function without the other. I'd longed for that same type of love once upon a time. Thought I'd found it, too. Turned out, my choice in a husband had been the sludge at the bottom of a dumpster—foul and repulsive. Oh, but he'd put on a good show to lure me in, a weak woman desperate for love.

But I wasn't loveable, nothing but a worthless whore.

My throat tightened again.

I am beautiful.

I am independent.

I am—

"I asked before hiring you if you were running from something," Annette said, her voice soft, and I forced myself to meet her probing gaze from across the store.

"I'm not."

She studied me with watery blue eyes while I forced myself to hold still. Finally, she nodded—same as the first time. "You need anything, don't hesitate to ask."

So many questions without actually asking them.

Swallowing, I nodded. "Thanks."

Annette didn't need to inquire when my reactions to a loud-mouthed asshole said it all. I suspected she'd seen right through me and would find ways to dig up my secrets and bring my past back when all I wanted to do was escape it.

Assholes like Davidson were the reason I was better off alone, I reminded myself while grabbing a bottle of glass cleaner off the shelf. But thoughts of Kane made me wish I'd found the strength to be vulnerable again, to trust not just another man, but my own self-esteem.

It seemed he and I both could do with a little healing.

Fucking accident scenes shot my nerves to shit every time dispatch sent me to one. A car had plowed into an elk, leaving the animal a mangled mess—alive —on the side of the road. Being the closest Game Warden, I made my way to the scene, steeling myself for the sight of crunched metal.

Blood and guts, no problem. Bent metal? My fucking kryptonite.

The accident had taken place a mile south of Kane's new place—my best friend I hadn't seen in years. He'd moved less than twenty miles from where we'd grown up, but he no longer frequented Jenny's Place, our old hangout and the only bar for miles. He didn't stop at the BI-LO for groceries every Sunday morning like he and Alana used to do, where I would happen to be shopping at the same time.

Intentionally because I'd needed Kane like I'd needed air —always had, always would.

My sister had claimed his heart, but I'd been too much of a chickenshit to tell him how I truly felt about him before she'd sunk her claws into him. Hiding my desire for my best friend in the sticks of Pennsylvania, where coming out of the closet would get my ass kicked, had frustrated the fucking hell out of me.

I'd joined the military to escape having to see them hang on each other. They'd married not long after I returned home from putting in my years. I settled in with Dad when cancer took Mom from us and contented myself with being home and having my best friend close by, but after the accident...

It had broken him, and I blamed myself, knowing I was unworthy of forgiveness in his eyes.

Kane had put up walls and changed everything about his way of life. He hardly even visited his parents. Last I'd spoken with him was the double funeral, where I'd fought off the sting of tears and the thickness in my throat when attempting to apologize. He'd ignored me, and I grieved more over losing him than my own sister. That's how I knew Kane would be the one I loved until I rested in my own grave.

Grief and self-blame continued to mix like a toxic brew in my soul—gut-wrenching, sickening—even though enough time had passed that they shouldn't. It had been their fight that sent her running to Dad's. Not my fault, but my heart couldn't let go of what I *had* been guilty of.

Alana had still been a shaking mess, but instead of forcing her to let me drive her back home in the thunderstorm, I agreed to her suggestion of following her instead. I'd seen her taillights shift like the tires were gliding sideways on wet pavement a second before lightning flashed.

The car had done a complete one-eighty in silence, the

headlights blinding me for a split second before it flew off the road. A crunching impact as the car had wrapped around a giant oak stopped my heart as quickly as it must have little Nat's in the back seat. Thunder had rumbled across the sky in weighty foreboding.

I couldn't remember calling 911, parking, or racing to the mangled car.

But the blood...

Alana's dazed eyes as she blinked at me, a crush of metal trapping her inside.

Little Nat.

Fuck.

I swallowed against the choking sadness that always hit whenever I remembered the sight of her. My niece hadn't suffered. A later autopsy confirmed that fact but didn't lessen my guilt over failing her.

Teeth clenched against the vividly colored memories, I rounded the bend and came upon the accident scene dispatch had informed me about. At least they'd said no human had been hurt by the impact. I kept my lights flashing atop my truck and pulled to a stop behind three vehicles lining the side of the road, one a cop car, the other a bystander a little farther up the road.

Four years in the military had taught me to keep my shit together on the outside, but that didn't stop my insides from twisting to the point of wanting to puke up the bagged dinner I'd downed an hour earlier.

Two cops stood talking to an elderly gentleman, one coming my way as I approached. I glanced at the elk beyond him, avoiding looking at the front end of the old man's car. The animal sat on its haunches, not making a sound.

"Pretty sure its hips are broken," the officer said. "Just got here and haven't had time to check it out."

Lips tight, I nodded, and we walked into the weeds where the animal had been thrown from the impact. No way in hell, the elk would be sitting there with two humans approaching if it could get up and go. No way in hell, the animal could be rehabbed, either.

"Gonna have to put it down," I told the officer beside me, frowning at the sight of the animal's twisted lower half.

"Damn. Old man is going to be upset."

"Maybe the fact the meat will go to the food bank for the needy will make him feel better," I said, turning away, sounding like a callous bastard, but unable to help myself. It was either that or lose my shit.

I went back to my truck and grabbed my M4 Carbine, loading it while walking through the greening weeds along the roadside, getting hold of my twisting stomach.

Less than a minute later, I called in the results of the accident, the no longer suffering animal loaded onto the back of my vehicle, and a tow truck backing up to the smashed-in car.

A truck approached from the opposite way, and I climbed back out of mine, my heart stalling out and kick-starting with a vengeance when I recognized the vehicle.

Kane.

I stood in front of my truck, hands fisted at my sides, my stomach once more churning, but for totally different reasons. I'd kept an eye on him from afar— fucking needed to see him living, breathing, so I could do the same. He'd never seen me. We'd never spoken, all because I feared the blame and rejection.

His truck slowed, and I held still, along with my lungs, watching as his head turned my way.

Our gazes connected, and time moved in slow motion, stealing my attempted inhale like a goddamn combat boot to my gut—hazel-green eyes I'd fought to keep from drowning in since I could remember, crooked nose from our one fight in high school, lips I'd dreamed of tasting...

My ears rang, and I shifted to hold contact with him until driving forced him to face forward. A few yards had separated us, but he'd never been able to keep his emotions off his face and out of his eyes.

Pain and longing—the same as the feelings coursing through me—not a trace of anger.

I turned fully, watching him slow even more.

Stop. Talk to me. Please.

His brake lights lit, and Kane pulled off the road, his truck idling, but he made no move to come to me.

I couldn't fucking stand it. It'd been five years too fucking long. I'd faced my fears in the military without being a chickenshit.

I can do the same right now.

Not wanting him to second guess himself over one moment of vulnerability, I hurried across the road and strode north, flexing my hands at my sides. While I'd have preferred going to the driver-side window, he hadn't pulled off the road far enough, so I opted for the passenger side. He rolled the window down as I approached, my heart in my throat.

Silence ruled for a few seconds as he came into view, our gazes locked tight as I pulled up alongside his truck.

Fuck, my heart melted all over again, same as when I'd seen him the first time in fifth grade. I'd known at that moment, all those years ago, I would love Kane Austin forever, but I'd known even then, attraction to the same sex sent people to hell. I'd had that hammered into my head by my over-righteous parents. I liked women, too. Kane just happened to own my heart. I'd since learned to think for myself, not believing the shit my parents and the man in the pulpit had spewed.

"Kane," I managed past the tight grip of need in my throat.

He nodded, his lips in a thin line, although his eyes only revealed his inner pain.

I wanted to ask a thousand questions, hold him in my arms, and try to take away the grief etched in the lines on his face that hadn't been there before I'd fucked up and let my sister drive home.

"I'm sorry," I spewed the two words I'd used at the funeral that hadn't gotten a response. "So fucking sorry ... it's my fault." Tears stung my eyes. "I killed Alana and Nat." My voice cut out, and I swallowed as his image wavered from the wetness coating my eyes.

"She made her choice," Kane finally said, his raspy voice like a goddamn breeze on a hot summer day.

"I should have made her let me take her home," I argued, my eyes pleading for him to tell me I wasn't at fault. I needed to hear those words, I needed his forgiveness.

Fuck, I needed *him*.

Kane huffed a sarcastic, pain-laced laugh. "Alana didn't obey anyone."

True, the rebellious little brat, but that truth didn't make me any less responsible for both our grief.

Silence returned, and longing for the old days damn near took out my knees—carefree and easy-going, hanging out and getting rip-roaring drunk, sharing women. Watching him fuck a woman while she sucked my dick, imagining it was his mouth on me rather than hers.

Before I'd found the balls to tell him the truth, my sister had caught his eye. No more sharing women, which had allowed me a step toward the intimacy with Kane I craved. Watching Alana on his lap, kissing lips I'd always longed to taste had always soured my stomach, but I hadn't been able to stop staring at the way his mouth moved over hers.

Kane's beard had filled in but didn't hide the full bottom lip I'd fantasized about biting, sucking.

Blood pumped into my dick for the first time in years.

Goddamnit.

I clenched my teeth and jerked my gaze back to his eyes. First time I saw him close enough to make out his face, and within seconds, my body goes from heartache to fucking. Knowing exactly how to turn off that goddamn switch, I focused on the feelings that had eaten away at my soul for five years.

I'd always wished Kane had been mine instead of Alana's, which doubled my fucking guilt over her death. Had I somehow turned the wheels of fate with wishful thinking? Had my jealousy, my fantasies, and my dreams of owning his heart been responsible for the accident that claimed two precious lives?

My twisting stomach erased all thoughts of tasting him.

"Fucking miss you," I whispered, my chest aching, my short fingernails digging into the palms clenched at my sides.

Kane hesitated. "Miss you, too," he murmured, turning his gaze forward as though looking away from me came easy. He clenched the steering wheel, and my gaze snagged on the string of beads around his left wrist.

Nat's...

He'd pulled it off her wrist that night and had clutched it to his chest as he sobbed in my arms while they cut apart the car to get to the bodies of Alana and Nat out of the wreckage.

So much left unsaid—so many wounds.

I couldn't turn away. Couldn't walk away...

"See you around." Kane put the truck in gear and pulled onto the road as though out for a Sunday drive. No stomping on the gas or tossing up pebbles alongside the road from beneath tires hell-bent on getting him the hell away from me.

No anger like I'd expected from the silence between us, but no forgiveness, either.

I hadn't bothered hiding the feelings in my eyes as I usually did, hadn't shut down the emotions wanting to overflow. I needed his forgiveness, but I wanted him under my hands, my mouth, almost as much.

Heart heavy, believing I would never have either, I turned away, catching sight of the old man's car from the front as the tow truck winched it up onto the bed.

Bent metal.

Cracked windshield.

Leaking radiator fluid.

My stomach heaved, but I managed to make it to my truck without puking up my guts. I focused on cleaning up the accident scene and filling out paperwork, details to finish my day, but I couldn't erase thoughts of Kane from my mind.

Having seen him face to face, I knew I didn't want to live without him anymore. Even if all I managed were words of forgiveness and a fraction of the friendship we'd once had, I would survive. I needed him like air, even tiny sips would keep my heart pumping.

I would find a way to make it happen or die trying.

KANE

Fate fucked with me.

The day from hell had to end with me seeing Charley for the first time since Alana and Nat's funeral. His familiar face, the emotions in his dark eyes, brought it all back just as strong as the storm earlier that morning, but a different sort of ache filled my heart. It wasn't grief, but pure heartache over losing the one person who knew me better than anyone—his dead twin included.

When I'd realized Charley's truck sat on the side of the road, my heart had sped up even as my foot let off the gas pedal.

I'd loved him first because I'd met him first. Seeing Charley in swim trunks had turned me on as much as Alana had in her bikinis. They both had been my people—mine to protect, mine to love, but only in the way our backwoods ways accepted.

Guilt over not giving Alana my whole heart had eaten away at me throughout our marriage, but I'd never wished I'd chosen differently. Alana had completed a part of me

Charley never could have, giving me the softness and gentle love I craved. She'd also given me the cutest daughter a man could wish for.

I eyed Nat's bracelet around my wrist while turning onto my long as hell driveway up the mountain. I'd had to restring it with a leather tie, so the beads weren't as tightly packed as when she'd had it around her tiny wrist, and I refused to take it off.

Seeing Charley, even speaking to him for all of those five minutes, had me toying with the beads as my thoughts scattered. His big brown eyes had been filled with pain.

Still.

Same as me.

He hadn't moved on.

Same as me.

Still lived with his dad, although my old father-in-law wasn't doing so well, last I'd heard. Heart problems, Annette had told me, and he refused treatment and surgery. I expected he was tired of living without his wife. I knew the feeling.

Charley didn't have a girlfriend, either, even though he was one hell of man—inside and out.

I'd wanted him in my arms so goddamn bad, so I'd left abruptly before losing control.

I parked in front of my woodshop and cut the engine, silence filling my cab.

I missed my best friend, ached to have him back in my life. Yes, seeing him had brought back memories, but not the sort that choked me with grief.

I had stayed away, wanting to move on with my life to forget the past, but seeing him... I realized I didn't want to move on completely. I'd missed out on five years of his friendship. Missed out on reminiscing, having someone to help me learn to laugh again—someone to lean on.

I rubbed a hand over my bearded jaw, heaved a sigh over even more regret to pile atop the shit in my heart, and climbed from my truck to unload the lumber I'd brought from work. Keeping busy wouldn't be hard, but keeping my thoughts occupied always proved a challenge. The day ran through my head while I worked, but my attention lingered on the two highlights, though the second had at first seemed shitty.

Jill Walters stirred my blood, and my conscious hated that fact.

I longed for Charley's presence but without the heartache first seeing him had brought.

Two hours later, I realized while sawing through a board, I hadn't thought about my wife and daughter most of the day. I also hadn't eaten dinner. My mind flitted from doe eyes to dark and back again, my dick twitching at thoughts of both. I expected even more guilt, but it seemed to have quieted as night filled the two windows outside my woodshop.

My cell rang, and I grabbed it off my workbench.

Charley.

Heart rate kicking up, I decided to answer, after five years of not seeing his familiar number on my screen.

"Charley," I rasped, my damn heart in my voice. I needed to tamp that shit down before he figured out the thoughts I'd carried toward him since fifth grade.

"Hey." He inhaled sharply. "So, I was thinking about heading to Jenny's Place Friday night. Want to grab a drink? Shoot some pool?"

Just like the old days.

My dick and lips twitched, and I almost smiled until I considered Friday and the forecast I'd heard on my way home.

"Bad storm's coming in," I said rather than accept his invite while tossing aside the hand plane I'd been using.

"They still affect you?" he asked, his voice quiet.

"Still." My lips pressed tight as I clenched my eyes shut, fighting off flashes of lightning, blood, and darkness.

He paused, and I didn't know how to fill the silence. I rubbed a hand down my face again, exhaling a steady breath.

"I'll drive?" Charley offered, his voice rising at the end of the sentence as though in question like a true Pennsylvanian.

I forced my eyelids open to focus on the board in front of me and the scent of fresh sawdust that usually soothed me. "Okay."

"Okay?"

I swallowed and wiped my damp palm down my work pants. "Yeah."

"Okay." He let out a breath of air that sounded like relief. "Pick you up at seven?"

"Sounds good."

I hung up, for the first time in forever excited about something. Wouldn't be able to stay out late because I planned to be at the Edwards to work on Saturday morning, but I was going to take that step toward attempting to live again.

My mind flitted back to Jill, the first woman I'd found attractive since Alana.

She was new to town.

I needed to get out more.

Maybe asking her out would help me move along, but first, I had to get through a stormy night out in public. Hopefully, having Charley at my side would make it bearable. Hopefully, Alana would send some sort of sign, telling me she didn't want me to remain a hermit, so I could take that step toward finding a new life for myself. One, unfortunately, couldn't include Charley in the way I would have preferred.

I HARDLY SLEPT Thursday night but from exhaustion rather than nightmares and storms. I looked forward to living again, even though how to do so kept my mind spinning into the early morning hours. Hanging with my best friend and maybe picking back up where we'd left off without the weirdness he had to have felt from me while we'd talked on the side of the road seemed a good place to start.

Seeing Jill again over at the store on Saturday, too.

Slowing, I drove by on my way home from work Friday afternoon, noting the concrete slabs had been poured, and the lumber I'd ordered had been delivered. I'd done the same every day since meeting Jill—slowing in hopes of catching a glimpse of her, even though doing so made me feel like a cheating bastard.

Alana stayed quiet from beyond the veil of death. No whispered words of encouragement or telling me to grab life by the balls and live it. No gentle breeze full of her laughter or Nat's.

Survivor's guilt was a bitch, but I couldn't resist the urge to breathe freely and see the glass as half-full as I used to.

It all seemed too much, too soon, but I needed it—wanted

it. I hoped Alana would forgive me, wherever she and Nat were, because I found myself ready, even without her approval. I hoped she wanted me to stop wasting my life and find happiness again, as my mom had been all over me to do —my reason for avoiding home.

At seven on the nose, I sat on my front porch in a rocking chair I'd made, waiting for Charley. Goddamn butterflies went to town in my stomach, something I hadn't felt since my wedding day. A shit ton of emotions rolled over me, and I struggled with what to focus on—guilt or excitement, Charley or Jill.

Realizing grief, my wife, and my daughter didn't linger at the top of that list was bittersweet.

More guilt swept in.

The crunch of tires on my dirt driveway and the rumble of a truck announced Charley's arrival, bringing my inner thoughts back to the present.

I stood and waited for him to round the bend, my heart thumping … dry mouth, too.

Get a grip, man.

I blew out a heavy exhale and shoved my hands in my jeans' pockets. His blue F250 came into view, and a hunger to see his face again, connect like we'd used to, had me swallowing a rush of saliva.

Fighting off a deep scowl, I kicked a pebble off my porch and followed after it down the stairs as Charley pulled to a stop. Steady steps took me toward the idling truck, but my nerves were shot to shit.

The click of his unlocking the doors hit my ears, and I pulled the passenger door open, finally looking at him.

Charley studied me with his dark-eyed gaze, a slight lift

at the corner of his lips dissolving the slight indent between my brows. "Hey."

"Hey." I tore my attention off him, the freshly shaved jawline I'd always thought was sexy as fuck, and climbed into his truck, buckling in. Not knowing what to do with my hands, I placed them on my thighs and turned back toward my best friend when he didn't drive off right away.

"It's my fault," Charley said, his gaze searching ... needing.

"You have my forgiveness if that's what you're looking for," I told him, my voice low.

He swallowed and nodded, a damn crack in his stoic facade. "Thank you."

"I never blamed you, though."

His brow furrowed. "Then why distance yourself?"

I exhaled another heavy breath. "I wanted to escape everything that reminded me of her. Them." I eyed my cabin, the supposed escape I'd built for myself. It hadn't given me what I'd wanted. "I thought by running, I could avoid grief."

"How's that working out for ya?" he asked with a crooked grin.

I snorted a laugh at one of his favorite lines I hadn't heard in years. "It isn't, asshole."

"Still fucking hurts." Charley searched my face as though looking for an answer, but he hadn't voiced a question.

"Still. I've been fucking aimless for too damn long," I spewed and clenched my jaw to keep my tight throat from welling my eyes.

Charley waited for me to voice my feelings like a damn shrink, but being vulnerable with him had always come easy. I knew he would never turn away from me.

"I haven't figured out where I belong with them gone," I rasped out, forcing my shoulders to relax.

"You belong here." Charley's non-nonsense tone from years in the military and with the Game Commission made itself known. "In my truck, hanging with me."

I searched for more in his eyes, a hint of similar feelings I always had for him, but all I saw was good old stoic Charley, my friend—*only* my friend.

"Tired of the daily grind without you," Charley continued when I couldn't find the words.

"Then we start over again." I held out my hand, and he clasped it tightly.

Energy crackled up my arm and straight to my dick. From lack of physical touch or more? I wasn't averse to finding out, but nothing in Charley's face or his body language suggested he might be on board as we fell back into time as though none had passed—as though heartache hadn't torn us apart.

Best to focus on Jill and give up dreams of loving him like I've always wanted to.

JILL

There's nothing better than fried food, especially the kind made at some backwoods bar, deep in the heart of no-man's-land. Steak fries and thick onion rings slathered in Heinz, a juicy burger alongside, and we're talking mouth-watering deliciousness I didn't usually partake in.

I had no wish to pack back on the pounds I'd gotten rid of.

Locals packed the bar and the dozen or so tables jammed into the hinky place. A few women sported eighties bangs, most in tight jeans and sleazy tops. I'd opted for comfy jeans and a loose sweater to ward against the cool spring night when Annette and Roy had insisted on taking me out to dinner.

Everyone knew everyone, those already drunk and laughing filled the bar with enough noise to drown out the jukebox beyond the pool tables behind us.

Old Jenny had opened the joint decades earlier when floating timber down the river had been the region's moneymaker. The place survived, eventually changing hands to her granddaughter a few years earlier.

That's what Annette told me, anyway. She knew everyone and everything about them. I cringed every time she introduced me to someone. So much for starting over with a quiet life, under the radar and inconspicuous. She treated me like the prized heifer in need of showing off.

"Oh." Annette's eyes twinkled as she peered over my shoulder. "Now, that is a man worth knowing."

"Leave the girl alone," Roy muttered, not for the first time, into his sweating beer mug.

"Jarod Johnson." Annette smiled at me. "About your age. Easy on the eyes. Single."

"Because he refuses to be tamed," Roy added. "Not good enough for our Jill."

Talk about warm fuzzies. I smiled, and Roy winked at me.

"Hush your mouth, Roy Edwards." Annette elbowed her husband, and I bit back a laugh while hunkering over my empty plate. "Jarod is running for local government," Annette continued.

"Then he's crooked, too," Roy shot out, clunking his empty mug onto the scratched wooden surface of the table.

"He has a spotless reputation and is as cute as a button," his wife argued.

I glanced over my shoulder for the hell of it, more to appease my friend before telling her Jarod Johnson wasn't my type. A couple of guys greeted a dark-haired man who appeared to have just entered.

"Is that him in the button-down and slacks?" I asked, *not* interested.

"Yes. Isn't he a dream?"

I snorted a laugh as the door opened, and Kane Austin filled the entry, stealing my oxygen. He stepped into Jenny's Place, his gaze quickly scanning our way. A few guys called out his name, grabbing his attention before his focus landed on our table.

Now, he *is a dream.* My insides fluttered.

"Well, I'll be damned," Annette said as my gaze slid to the man walking in behind Kane—taller, his hair a tad more dirty blond, but no less hot than Kane. Dark eyes and a content smile on his face, he watched others greet the man he trailed after.

A tiny blonde let out a shriek and launched herself into Kane's arms, her legs wrapping around his waist like she belonged on him or some such shit. Her tinkling laughter annoyed the hell out of me. I scowled as ugly jealousy wrapped itself around my stomach and squeezed. I had no right but couldn't help the instantaneous flare-up, seeing his hands on her thighs.

Kane's beard twitched as though he clenched his jaw, and he moved his face away from her as she tried to kiss him. His disinterest made me feel the slightest bit better, but I still hated the fact she clung to him.

"Stupid girl," Annette muttered behind me. "First time he's out in public … let the man breathe."

I had to agree. He tried to set her aside, but she wiggled and pressed in tighter, peering up at him with a drunken smile. My gaze flitted to the man behind Kane, who watched the woman's antics with a thoughtful expression—a reserved, hot-as-hell man.

"Humph."

I glanced back at Annette quickly, all sorts of pleasant

zings shooting across my skin from the two men, even as pissiness over the brazen woman's actions sizzled my blood.

Lips pursed in a wrinkly frown, she peered across the bar. "She and Kane were an item for some time, but once Kane set his eyes on Alana, that little slut took a back seat."

Slut? I bit back a smirk, soaking in Annette's gossip.

"She wasn't good enough for him then, she's not good enough for him now," Annette stated with finality.

"Who's the man with him?" I couldn't help my curiosity about the equally hot guy.

"Charley Woodhill. Those boys haven't been seen together for five years. They used to be best friends before the accident." Annette's eyes moved as though tracking them, and I hoped like hell Kane had rid himself of that little *slut*.

"Charley's twin was Kane's wife," Roy told me, his focus on the pair as well.

"Rumors filled everyone's lips, there'd been a falling out. Blame. Guilt." Annette shrugged and turned back toward me while I processed her words. "Kane and Alana fought, she ran off to her dad's house, and Charley talked her into heading back home. Their dad told me she'd been pretty upset but refused to allow Charley to drive her."

Best friends, Kane married his sister, sister dies, and they aren't seen in public for five years... I expected the rumors of a fallout were right. I bet Annette had hit the nail on the head. Blame and guilt do nothing but rip up a person's insides and wreak havoc on emotions.

The two men moved into my line of sight, hanging at the back of the bar—minus one blonde leech, thank goodness. Charley stood back while others chatted with Kane, a bottle of beer in his hand, his gaze locked on his friend's face.

Kane's smile appeared forced, but recognizing discomfort came easy since the feeling rooted deep inside me. He glanced toward our table, catching me staring as Annette rattled on with gossip about the two boys breaking hearts across the county before Kane had settled down. The beginnings of a smile hinted at his lips, the first bit of happiness I'd seen on his face since meeting him earlier in the week.

He raised his bottle in greeting.

Heat flushing my body and face, I smiled, nodded, and quickly turned away. Those bedroom eyes, kissable, full lips, shoulders stretching his flannel tight across broad shoulders... I didn't need any more fuel for my fantasies, thank you very much.

Annette's steady gaze drew my attention, her painted eyebrows rising. "He caught your eye, has he?"

"No," I replied too quickly, sending even more heat to my cheeks. My gaze flitted his way again but snagged on his friend.

Charley, stoic and seemingly self-assured, reminded me of a cop with his rigid stance, confident and watchful. *Not my favorite people since they'd failed to protect me from JD.*

As though feeling my stare, he turned his head, his gaze directly on me. More of those zings raced straight between my thighs, and my pulse took to a happy, tripping dance.

Lack of sex? Estrogen spike? I wasn't sure what messed with my body, but I'd never felt such a force before—pulled in two different directions, a strong attraction to two men.

Losing myself in Charley's dark eyes, I wondered about *him.* How he grieved for his sister and niece—if he still did. He'd lost his best friend for years, too, from what Annette had said, but it seemed the two men had found peace between them.

I found myself smiling, happy for him—for both of them.

Kane elbowed Charley, and we both looked at Kane. He glanced at me, then back at Charley again. His lips moved, but I couldn't hear over the voices and the new country song kicking in the jukebox behind us. Something about a hurricane and storms like the one dumping rain outside the bar's windows.

Kane motioned our way with his head, and the two men started over, sending my heart into hyperdrive. My gaze flitted from one to the other, wanting to soak in the sight of each of them, while I fought to keep from shifting in my chair.

Annette sat back in hers, calm as could be, a Cheshire cat smile on her face. "Well, hello, boys," she greeted them. "The famous dangerous duo. Good to see you out and about together again."

Charley chuckled, his gaze flitting my way as my stomach flipped over the deep rumble in his chest. So, maybe not as stoic as I'd first thought.

Kane smiled, his attention fixed on me while I sat like a deer in headlights, the focus of two hot-as-hell men plastered on me, flipping my insides.

Kane smiled. I'd found him beautiful before, but...

The deep sadness of a shattered soul didn't haunt his eyes at that moment, but my heart ached for him all the same.

"Charley, this is Jill. She works for us at the store," Roy said, surprising me, he beat his matchmaking wife to introductions. She'd probably been too caught up in watching the three of us ogling one another.

Charley stuck out his hand while stepping closer, jerking my attention off Kane.

I responded on autopilot, biting back a gasp as Charley's warm palm slid against mine, and the scent of sandalwood wafted over me.

Strong, firm, and softer than I'd expected for such a big man, and lordy, did he smell delicious.

"Jill," he murmured in his deep voice, his gaze flitting across my face and keeping those sweet tingles alive and well.

"Charley," I replied breathlessly. *Damnit.* I shot a quick glance at Kane, who sipped his beer and watched Charley.

"Pleasure to meet you." Charley's murmur of the word *pleasure* sending a shiver along my spine and raising the hairs on my arms. My nipples hardened to points, and I hunched my shoulders in an attempt to hide his effect on me.

"You, too," I managed to choke out, totally out of my element. A hot, bothered mess by a couple of best friends … hot friends—sinfully so.

Whore.

I grimaced and swallowed at the echoed memory, jerking my focus back to my empty plate.

Annette let out a sigh. "Looks like your old pool table opened up. We won't keep you."

They moved off in my periphery, and I couldn't keep from glancing after them. Tight-fitting jeans on both encased asses a woman could sink her teeth into and wide, strong shoulders to carry the weight of the world.

"Goodness." Annette let out a quiet huff of laughter. "Jill, I swear you're going to turn this town upside down with all the eyes you're getting tonight."

I tore my attention from Kane and Charley, my face hot again as I glanced between her and her husband. "So, what are your plans for that old garden bed out back of your house?" My voice shook, but at least I hadn't taken off like a fox with its tail on fire.

Roy perked up, a twinkle in his heavy-lidded eyes. "That small bit of land was my pride and joy. Old knees keep me from it now, but if you want to take it over, the fresh produce lit off the shelves like a deer to barking dogs."

I forced a laugh even as my mind strayed to the two men in my periphery.

The clatter of breaking balls sounded, and Charley snorted a curse. "Five fucking years without playing, and you can still sink two balls on the break."

"Good hands," Kane replied to his friend, a smile in his raspy voice.

I clenched my thighs together at the thought of those hands on me.

"Zucchini," Roy said, and I fought to focus on the light in his eyes and the conversation I'd started. "Too late to start our own tomatoes from seed, but we can get some from Landry's greenhouse. They have a nice organic section."

"If you're starting up that garden," Annette said, causing me to blink away the image in my head of Kane's hands on me, "then I want radishes and beets."

They bantered back and forth a bit with ideas while I nodded, adding my two cents when asked. Yes, I would tend the garden. Yes, I'd done a bit of gardening back in Maryland before moving north.

At least they didn't question my old home. I guessed my

tight-lipped, vague answers in the previous two weeks had been hint enough, I didn't wish to speak of my past.

I caught bits and pieces of the reminiscing going on behind me, Charley's lower timbre sometimes getting lost in the jukebox music. Kane actually laughed once, and my lips responded as happiness for him swept over me.

Grief sucked. It took me over a decade to start living again after my parents passed within six months of one another. Cancer took them both, leaving me alone in the world in my early twenties. I had been sucked into JD's world when he'd offered comfort. Had I known the man on the inside didn't match the facade he portrayed, I never would have walked willingly into his arms.

"Kane will be over in the morning," Annette reminded Roy, but I hadn't forgotten.

A concrete truck had shown up earlier that morning and poured the two slabs beyond the three standing cabins. Roy had told me Kane would build cabins atop, identical to the others, and would start the next day.

The garden would give me an excuse to be outside, enjoying the view of the beautiful lumberjack when not working.

Annette glanced at me.

"What?" My face heated again as she narrowed her watery gaze.

"Seeing that young man out again makes me think he's finally ready to move on." Her tone hinted at what she really meant.

I glanced over at Kane. Couldn't help the draw he had—both men—had on me. Kane leaned over to shoot, and Charley's gaze dropped to his backside. Couldn't blame the man for doing so, and seeing the lust in his eyes sent all kinds of delicious naughty thoughts through my imagination. A man didn't look at someone's ass like that unless they wanted it.

Instead of getting jealous like I'd done over that slut climbing Kane like a tree, Charley's lust for his friend made me burn with need all the more. Shifting on my chair didn't relieve the ache between my thighs.

"Leave the girl alone," Roy repeated, pushing himself to his feet with his cane. "I'm ready for my bed."

I tore my attention off Charley's face and stood as Annette did.

"Roy Edwards!" she squeaked when Roy pinched her backside.

"Yes, dear?" He laughed, switching his cane to his right hand.

She chuckled through pursed, wrinkled lips and took his outstretched arm. Lovebirds even after almost sixty years together. To find that kind of love...

My entire backside lit with flame, the hairs on my nape standing on end. Glancing over my shoulder, I found Kane and Charley watching me from opposite ends of the pool table. I couldn't decide who looked hotter in their jeans or who had me thinking between-the-sheets thoughts.

My fantasies of old—the ones I'd always felt guilty over most whenever JD had accused me of being unfaithful to him —lit with vivid clarity in my mind.

Forget Charley on Kane fantasies. I wanted a Kane, Jill, and Charley sandwich.

Lordy, yes, please.

Gulping, I turned forward once more, tripping in my

haste to catch up with the Edwards. If I wasn't careful, I could wind up in even more trouble than I'd escaped. Panties shouldn't soak so easily. Fantasies like the ones in my mind existed in naughty paperbacks and never became real life.

But I couldn't keep my mind from wishing for that very thing.

Gracie had hopped onto Kane as though it hadn't been fifteen years since she'd had his dick inside her pussy while I fucked her ass. Seeing her hang on him like that brought back memories of sharing her and the handful of other women we'd reeled in.

I'd always been the instigator when it came to threesomes because having a woman between us was as close as I would get to intimacy with the one man I wanted. I'd never been attracted to another man—just Kane.

One simple conversation, one act of forgiveness, had made right what I hadn't dreamed possible. I had his but would never forgive myself.

We'd settled back into our friendship as though a day hadn't passed, and I'd never felt so damn relieved. Having Kane beside me, hearing his rasped voice, healed the piece of me that had been torn from my soul.

Learning how he'd filled his time by making furniture made me fucking proud. Kane hadn't taken to the bottle like his father had in his younger years. He also hadn't fucked another woman, hadn't even been out, confirming the rumors I'd heard.

He warned me two beers might put him on his ass, but I promised to see him home safely.

Seeing Gracie on him, though, had my mind going straight to a threesome, even if she no longer got my dick hard. I'd give her a go if she offered, just to be close to Kane, to latch onto his gaze as we'd always done when sharing women. I imagined the pussy or ass as his body every time while losing myself in his eyes.

Had he ever done the same?

Lips in a thin line, he set Gracie aside, snuffing out thoughts of ending our night with her between us. She shot me a pout, and I shrugged, following Kane toward the bar's end.

A couple guys we used to hang with handed us cold ones, and I stood back and watched Kane reacquaint himself with life, society, friends, and laughter. The rain started outside, but enough noise rose inside to drown out the thunder.

It only took about ten minutes for Kane's shoulders to relax, but hints of his gorgeous grin twitched the clipped beard along his jaw. I wanted to feel his whiskers rubbing my face … my skin.

He lifted his glass in greeting to someone across the bar, and I studied his profile—heavy brow, deep-set greenish eyes that always darkened when he got hard, the lips I'd dreamed of devouring.

Talking down my dick didn't come easy, so I forced my focus off him. Awareness of being watched turned my head in the direction I felt called to look.

A brunette I didn't recognize sat with the Edwards. Lips

parted, she stared at me. Not a stitch of makeup painted her face, and her straight, silky hair hung down over her shoulders. Perfectly arched eyebrows and a pointy chin made for biting held my attention.

Goddamn.

The urge to adjust my swelling dick twitched my fingers. I clutched my beer bottle tighter.

An elbow to my arm jerked me around, and I found Kane eyeing me. He glanced at her and eyed me again.

"What? I can't check out a hot woman?" I joked, wishing like fuck he'd say he didn't want his man looking at anyone but him.

"Have you met her?" he asked instead, and I shook my head. "Her name is Jill. She's been working for the Edwards for a couple of weeks now."

"She's fucking hot."

"Come on." He motioned toward their table. "I'll introduce you."

He knew her. Had they spoken, or was it Annette who'd filled him in? I wondered if he was as hard for her as I was. Being new to town, she'd want to make friends. If she was Kane's choice for the night, I sure as fuck wouldn't say no, even though parts deep inside my heart didn't want to share him. That might change once I got to know her, though. Fuck knew, she put off vibes that licked fire over my skin.

Jill's attention snapped between the two of us as we approached, her face easy as pie to read. Interested, without a doubt, but wariness closed her off. She didn't want attention. At least her mind didn't—her straining nipples stated otherwise.

Old man Roy ended up introducing us, but I barely heard

him over the buzz in my ears. It's as if something inside her called to me, just like I'd felt her stare. Her palm against mine hit my groin like a shot of one of those instant energy drinks, making me uncomfortable as fuck in my jeans.

A woman who turned me on all on her own, with no help from Kane—I wasn't sure what to make of that. I'd fucked women over the years but not out of attraction, only need.

She turned away as though my full attention burned, and I glanced at Kane.

He stared at her like a starved man, and my heart fell. Swallowing against the disappointment over never having him, reiterated, but I straightened my shoulders and dealt with it like a man. Same as before, I would step back and let Kane find his happiness.

Unless he wanted to share...

If not, I would content myself with being friends. Waiting for him to decide, waiting for him to initiate something with her would fucking kill, but if the possible outcome of the three of us being together lay in our future, it would be worth every goddamn second.

My dick didn't like having to wait, but I would do anything for Kane Austin—fucking anything.

We moved off to play pool, exactly as planned for the night, and the waiting *did* suck. I decided it wouldn't hurt to plant a seed or two, see where Kane's head was.

"Gracie wanted to pick right back up where we'd left off," I said, leaning down to break for our second game.

"Not interested," Kane muttered, watching as I sank a striped ball.

"What about Jill?" I asked quietly, rounding the table to decide on my next shot. The jukebox spewed shitty music behind us, but I didn't need said woman and the Edwards overhearing our conversation.

"What about her?"

"You seem interested in *her*." I banked a shot and sank another ball without Kane replying.

He glanced at Jill, and that glint I recognized returned, only to be snuffed out by guilt as he tore his focus from her. He'd never been good at hiding his emotions.

"It's okay to put yourself back out there again, Kane." I straightened, holding my stick out in front of me, waiting as he glanced at her again as they all stood to leave, the war so damn obvious, I hurt for him.

Jill glanced over her shoulder at us, gaze flitting one to the other. No doubt, the woman was on board—so was my dick. She stumbled in her rush to catch up to the Edwards, endearing her to me.

"She's the first woman to get my attention," Kane said once the door shut behind her, returning his attention to our game. "Makes me feel like a fucking cheat."

"My sister wouldn't want you to hide away. She'd want you to be happy."

Kane made a shot and straightened again, eyeing the table.

"Are you?" I asked.

"Happy?" He grabbed the chalk without glancing at me.

"Yeah."

He chalked up good before answering. "No."

"Then go after what makes you happy."

Kane glanced over at the door Jill had disappeared through.

"You don't need my permission," I said quietly, "and even though I just got you back, I won't *hold* you back."

Kane studied me long enough, I almost shifted my stance, but I held still, face blank as hell. "Not sure I'm ready," he said.

"You can hang with me, then," I said with a grin, my breath almost leaving in a rush. "Fuck knows, I don't mind having you around."

He snorted. "You were around for *everything* until Alana."

I eyed my friend, considering what he meant, my dick more than happy with the train I hoped his mind hopped aboard. "I could be again if you're just looking to have some fun."

He smirked, the sight so goddamn hot, I had to clench my jaw to keep from groaning. "We had some good times," he said, no trace of grief or pain in his eyes.

"Fucking right, we did," I agreed.

"Miss those times, too."

Fuck, if he only knew...

"Yeah," I managed, my gaze dropping to his ass again as he leaned over the table. Balls aching, I flagged down a waitress. I could easily handle another beer and still, drive home later. Might as well get my buzz going to get through the next couple of hours without giving in to the need to hold him down over the table and take what I dreamed belonged to me.

"Trying to get me drunk?" Kane asked when I clinked a cold one against his.

"Damn right," I joked with a wink.

He put his lips on the bottle, and I turned away before he realized I only half-joked.

I GOT HIM DRUNK, alright. Had to help him into my truck at midnight and listen to his ass laugh about shit we'd done as kids while heading back to his place. At least all the beer he drank didn't have him breaking down in grief.

Whatever storm promised to overshadow the night hadn't even been an issue while we were at Jenny's. The roads were wet, but the moon peeked between clouds creating a sheen along the blacktop.

I had blue balls from fucking hell, but I'd laughed more in one night than I had in the previous five years. Kane made breathing easier, his smiling eyes a smooth shot of whiskey to my parched throat.

I pulled in front of his small cabin, put the truck in park, and turned toward my friend, not near ready for the night to end.

Kane fumbled with his seatbelt, then fumbled with the door handle.

Chuckling, I cut the engine and climbed out, happy to have the excuse to see him inside. "Come on, big boy." I pulled him from the truck and slung his arm over my shoulder.

"Drank too much," he slurred with a big ass grin, his breath reeking of hops.

"How's that working out for ya?"

"Fuck off, Charley."

I chuckled, our boots thumping on the three stairs leading to the porch, and Kane let out a sigh.

"I did good with this place, huh?"

"Yeah, Kane, you did," I agreed, opening the unlocked front door.

The moon shed enough light through the two windows flanking the door, I could make out the small living area. I unwound his arm from my shoulders. "Got any lights in this fucking place?"

Kane leaned against the wall with a groan, his hand searching the wooden logs. Overhead lights flicked on. He hadn't been kidding about the homemade furniture. Looked like expensive shit out of a catalogue from New England or something.

"Shit, Kane, you ought to be selling this—"

"I'm fucking smashed." Kane let out a chuckle and thudded into me while attempting to walk.

I grabbed his arm again, saving the conversation of his wasted talents for another time. "Bedroom?"

"Back there."

I headed toward the only door in the open concept area and nudged it with my foot before trying to wrangle my noodle-like friend inside.

He slumped on the bed's edge, and I dropped to my knees to take off his boots.

I'm at Kane's knees.

My fucking fingers trembled as I yanked at the knots of his boots' laces.

"Gets lonely in here," he muttered, his hands lax on his thighs as I tugged his boots off. Sadness filled his voice, and I clenched my jaw in order to lift my focus to his face.

He stared out the dark window.

I could take away his loneliness, but I didn't deserve that gift. But if...

Would he even want me? Would the thought of being with me sicken him as it would the conservative right-wingers living around us? Never mind the fact he'd been married to my sister and shared her bed for years.

"Go on and lie down," I muttered while standing, too many truths shutting down my rising hope.

He tugged at his shirt, his brow furrowed and lips pursed.

Shaking my head, I reached out to help him and tossed the shirt aside.

Holy fucking mother of God.

Kane hadn't let himself go. Muscles rippled where they hadn't before with bulges and indents to make any human salivate for a taste.

He fell back, eyes closing, his fingers on the button of his jeans.

"Need help?" I asked, my voice ragged as hell and rumbling deep inside my chest.

"Yeah."

Fuck.

Teeth clenched, my dick hard as steel, I tried to keep my fingers off his skin while helping him shed the jeans that clung to his ass like a goddamn glove. At least he wore boxer briefs, so I wasn't tempted to linger, checking him out.

Kane's lips curled as he scooted up and his head landed on his pillow. Dark lashes shadowing his cheeks, he let out another sigh. "You gonna tuck me in and kiss me good night, too?" he asked.

I threw a blanket over him. "Shut the fuck up," I muttered, my lips tingling and fingers twitching to take advantage of his drunkenness. I stalked off toward the open doorway on the room's far side and found a bathroom as expected. The medicine cabinet held pain killers, but I had to retrieve a cup from the kitchen.

Kane passed out before I returned, so I placed the pills and water on his bed stand. Lips parted, he breathed heavily. I stared for a few seconds, so damn tempted to taste them...

"Go ahead," Kane whispered, even though I'd have bet money he slept.

My head tipped to the side, unsure what he'd meant. Rather than fuck up, I opted to *go ahead* and leave him be.

You got your best friend back. Don't be a greedy bastard.

We'd rebuilt the bridge, but I would have to be patient for the highway beyond. While I wished for more than we'd had before Alana, I couldn't bring myself to hope. Life's roads weren't free of bumps, and storms of life battered and bruised hearts.

We both knew that all too well.

KANE

*M*y fucking head.

Scowling, I grabbed the two white pills off my bed stand and chased them with the glass of room temperature water beside them.

Charley, always the caretaker. He'd seen me home safely, just like he'd promised. He'd tried to do the same with Alana, but I never once blamed him for the accident. Offering forgiveness, when I didn't think he needed it, seemed to be what he'd wanted to hear, though. Spending the night with him reminiscing had been the highlight of the previous five years of my life, even if my temples throbbed, and my still-parched throat wanted more of him—his laughter, his nearness.

I glanced at my clock—seven-fifteen. I didn't have to be at the Edwards' until eight.

Exhaling, I laid back again and closed my eyes.

The attraction I'd felt for Charley hadn't changed or diminished. The familiar sandalwood scent of him had brought comfort—and lust. Being enclosed in his cab when he'd picked me up had brought on a semi I'd dealt with all damn night. The only flagging moment was when Gracie climbed me like a coon up a goddamn tree—drunk bitch. Yeah, Charley and I had shared her a few times, but that had ended when I'd decided Alana was it for me. All those years passed and Gracie thinks the second I step back into what society we had, we would pick up where we'd left off? I didn't even know the woman anymore. Sure as fuck didn't get a rise out of her tiny body all over mine, either. Made my damn skin crawl.

But Jill.

My lips twitched along with my dick's temptation to rise with the sun. Fuck, it'd been too long since I'd sported morning wood. No fucking doubt, her body was on board for what definitely brewed between us—pebbled nipples, huge as hell pupils, parted lips. I'd caught her checking Charley out, too.

Fucking Charley.

My dick swelled fully, and I shoved down my boxers, groaning as I palmed my hard length. It'd been too long since I'd jerked off. A few slow strokes and pre-cum oozing made one hell of a mess in my palm.

"Fuck." Teeth clenched, I tipped my head back and forced myself to go slow, squeezing tight at the base every time my balls tingled, ready to blow. Images of Jill and Charley flashed through my mind, keeping me on the edge—her back arched beneath me, Charley watching me fuck her with his hands on my body, her lips on mine, burying my dick deep inside her warmth … Charley burrowed inside me.

A deep groan spilled from me at the first shot of spunk up over my chest, fucking hit my chin. Curses rang out in my silent bedroom as the rest followed, ropes of white, striping my upper body with every grunt tightening my abs. Went on for a fucking eternity, but goddamn, did the release ease my body.

I heaved for breath, and my heart pounded as if I'd run up a mountainside. Never felt so relaxed, though. Felt good, but not quite good *enough.* I wanted more—flesh to touch, lips to taste, shared breaths—connection instead of loneliness.

"Fuck." I tossed my arm over my eyes and laid there, holding my softened dick until my breathing leveled out, not experiencing the guilt I'd expected over my first morning jerk off in five years—yes, five fucking years.

Would you mind if I moved on?

The thought floated through me, and I strained to hear Alana's answer, a hint of suggestion in my mind.

My cell buzzed on the bed stand, and with a curse over being distracted from a possible conversation with my dead wife from the grave, I grabbed it with my free hand.

Charley: **Hungover?**

I relaxed back against my pillow, texting one-handed since spunk covered my right hand.

Me: **Fuck, yeah.**

I could imagine he laughed at my reply.

Charley: **At least I didn't take advantage of you.**

I remembered muttering for him to go ahead the night before—but he'd left. Had I meant for him to kiss me good-night before tucking me in? Fuck, yeah, I did. Temptation to text back I wished he *had* taken advantage of me shook my hand as I considered how to reply.

I just fucked my hand while thinking about you.

There's sticky white shit all over my chest because of you.

I'd have given you everything if you had stayed.

"Fuck." I closed my eyes again and stroked the semi the thoughts of giving myself to him brought back to life. The cell buzzed in my hand before I could figure out what I could say that wouldn't be weird as fuck and ruin the friendship I'd found again.

Charley: **Let me know when you're ready for another night on the town.**

A true chickenshit, I sent him a thumbs up, exhaled a heavy huff, and rolled off the bed, holding my hard, slick cock.

Shower, blow another load, coffee, then off to the Edwards' for a day of work with the very real possibility of catching an eyeful of Jill.

At least everyone in our county wouldn't look at me like I had three heads if I decided to ask her out. Not that she was second best in my mind. Fuck knew, the idea of her set me off as much as Charley. She was just the safer choice—as Alana had been.

Guilt over finding Jill attractive and jerking off to thoughts of her and Charley didn't churn my guts or plague my head. Happiness, excitement for the day, rose instead.

I stood by my front window, watching the sun crest the trees while sipping my coffee, the silence not as lonely as the week before. No clouds threatened, no dark shadows hung on the horizon.

Perhaps healing wasn't as impossible as I'd thought.

~

I LOADED up my tools in my truck at ten of eight and made it down the mountain in five minutes. I took my time unloading and setting up plywood atop horses to act as a workbench, a few too many butterflies in my gut, trying to keep the noise level down since the Edwards' cabins were rented out.

A little after eight-thirty, I got to work, any movement in my periphery speeding up my heart and drawing my attention off the sill plate I attached to the first concrete slab.

No Jill.

Birds chirped their hearts out as the sun fully crested the mountain behind me, glinting beams off the dew covering the pines to my right. The guests stirred in the cabins, and two of the renters hunched in sweatshirts hurried toward the campers' bathrooms at the back of the store.

A few vehicles sped past, but the sounds of slapping footfalls and awareness turned me fully around.

Jill jogged into the parking lot, stealing my breath.

Her hair was pulled up in a messy ponytail. Running shorts barely covered her ass, and her long, shapely legs twitched my dick to life again at the thought of having them wrapped around me.

I straightened, hammer in hand, and watched her approach, her head swiveling my way. Face flushed and dripping with sweat, she slowed to a walk, her smile damn near putting me on my ass. I stared like a perv and couldn't find my lips to return her smile, she had me so damn tied up in knots.

"Hey," she said, breathless as fuck, her lush tits heaving as she sucked in oxygen.

I clenched my jaw to keep from groaning. "Hey," I managed to rasp out.

She bent at the waist, hands on her knees, but continued to peer up at me. "It looked like you were having a good time last night."

I nodded. "My first time out in a long time."

"So Annette said."

My lips curled upward. "If you ever need to know anything about anyone, she's got you covered."

Jill's breathless laughter eased the knot in my stomach, and I found my smile coming easier. "She loves to talk, that's for sure."

"She does." I glanced at the store, fully expecting to find Annette in one of the store windows, her hawk eye on us.

"Is she watching?"

I laughed, moving my attention back to Jill. "Not that I could see, but knowing Annette..."

Her light brown eyes filled with a lightness, carefree compared to the two times I'd seen her before, not as wary, not as closed off—fucking beautiful. "Yeah. Hawk eye." She glanced over her shoulder, and I stole the time to take in a quick eyeful.

Her frumpy t-shirt didn't hide the roundness of her breasts or hardened nipples beneath. At least the shirt ended at her waist, not covering the swell of her hips and juicy ass.

Fine as fuck.

She cleared her throat, and I jerked my focus back to her face. Her raised eyebrow heated my own goddamn face, and I lifted my hammer, grasping the worn, wooden handle.

"Guess I'll get back to work," I tossed out, feeling like a goddamn teenager, caught checking her out.

"Want a coffee?" Jill's soft smile eased my embarrassment.

I'd already had two after my too-long shower, but I wasn't going to pass up the opportunity to have her company for a few extra minutes.

"Sure."

"Black?" she asked.

"How'd you know? Annette?"

"No." A droplet of sweat slid down her temple. "Looking at you … manly lumberjack type." She shrugged. "Milk and sugar just don't come to mind."

I wondered what *did* come to mind as I stared at her mouth a second too long.

Jill turned her head away, licking her lower lip.

Goddamn. "Coffee would be great," I offered her an excuse to escape.

With a quick glance and uneasy smile, she trotted off toward the store.

Yeah, my focus dropped to her ass. My dick swelled, and the second she disappeared inside the back door, I turned and adjusted myself. Guess my dick had enough sleeping and grief. The relentless fucker seemed ready to make up for lost time.

I exerted more strength than necessary nailing two-by-fours together, hoping to talk myself down, but awareness of Jill's presence behind me a few minutes later brought it right the fuck back. Keeping my lower half turned away, I accepted the coffee she held out.

Our fingers brushed, and her breath caught.

"Thanks," I mumbled after unclenching my jaw.

She took off like a rabbit, loping for the stairs leading to her apartment above the store.

Fuck, fuck, fuck.

I gulped the hot coffee, enjoying how it hit my empty stomach with a searing burn, watching her ass flex as she climbed the stairs. One last curse under my breath as she disappeared inside.

Annette stood in the back window watching me—of course. I lifted one hand in a wave and turned away. It was going to be one hell of a long day.

Annette moseyed over an hour later with fresh baked muffins and another coffee—of course. "Good to see you out last night, Kane."

"It was good to be out." I sat on the second slab and wiped the sweat off my forehead with my sleeve before shoving half the blueberry muffin in my mouth. I knew she wouldn't walk away without the whole scoop, and she didn't disappoint the second she settled onto the concrete beside me.

"So, you and Charley finally patched things up?"

I hadn't felt like there was anything to patch up, but I nodded while chewing.

"Good." She nodded, too. "Alana would want that."

My throat tightened, and I glanced out over the mountain with its leafing trees, attempting to hide the brown leaf litter below.

"She would," I agreed, lifting my attention to the bright blue sky and the sun that had burned the dew away.

"That boy hasn't been the same without you in his life."

I studied the old woman's face, wondering about her meddling. Did she see more than friendship bonded me and Charley, as far as I was concerned? She certainly wasn't disgusted if her soft smile indicated her thoughts about the possibility.

"How so?" I couldn't help but ask.

"I've seen him around, moping, feet dragging. He's stopped in dozens of times over the years to ask after you. I'd watch him head back to his truck, and every time, he looked up the mountain at the road leading to your cabin. Anyone with half a brain could see he was missing you."

I shoved the other half of the muffin in my mouth and chewed, waiting her out, wondering what other goodies—fucking hoping—she might offer unintentionally or otherwise. She didn't disappoint.

"And last night? Charley followed you like a lost puppy. I swear that boy loves you as much as his sister did."

My damn throat closed off as my heart thumped in my ears. Did he truly, or was the town gossip's age finally affecting her brain?

Jill's door pulled open, her gaze landing on me as she shut it behind her, robbing my thoughts. We watched one another as she descended, and the side of my face tingled beneath Annette's study.

"You went from no one to two someones overnight."

I jerked my head back toward Annette, and she studied my face, unsmiling.

"I know you two boys sowed your wild oats back in the day, but you can't be doing that with her, Kane Austin. Charley will do whatever you ask, so I'm begging you to choose one or the other. She seems to be sweet on both of you. Don't take advantage of that, and don't hurt my girl."

Fuck. I swallowed and nodded. What else could I do? Annette knew more than was good for her, but maybe it was good for everyone as a whole to do as she said.

She patted my arm and pushed up, muttering something

about old bones. "She's got some heavy secrets, that girl. Best be mindful of that when deciding who you'll give your heart to this time around."

"Not sure I have much of a heart left."

"Pshaw." She made a humph noise in her throat. "You're *all* heart, boy, and it's high time you shared all that love inside you again."

Annette moved off toward the store, waving at Jill, who let herself into the fenced-in garden area Roy used to practically live in before the stroke two years earlier slowed his lifestyle to puttering around their house.

I slugged down some hot-as-hell coffee and turned away, instead of filling my eyes with Jill Walters, new-to-town stranger, who had some heavy secrets, according to Annette. I'd seen the wariness in her eyes and got the sense she didn't trust men.

The thought someone had hurt her, that she had moved up to the mountains to try escape grief and pain, only heightened that sense of protectiveness I'd felt when first meeting her. It drew me toward her even more, a shared connection of sorts.

Charley would never need me in that way. That stoic bastard could stand on his own two feet without any help.

While I didn't feel I had a heart left to give, it felt torn in two. I ached for Charley, but I couldn't keep my eyes off Jill.

Toiling in that garden.

Climbing the stairs to her apartment.

Wondering at her past, her pain, and her secrets.

Catching her eye, her flushed face and quick glances away twitched my dick every damn time.

Late afternoon, she brought me a bottled water, not

meeting my gaze like she had after her jog. It's like the early morning run had freed her from whatever haunted her mind for a short time. Cheeks pink, she flitted her attention over my bare chest as though the sight of me burned her eyes.

"Thanks." I chugged the water down in one go, the cold going clear to my stomach. The sun had turned up the heat, feeling more like a summer day than early spring. I'd shed my shirt around noon, hating to have sweat-soaked cotton sticking to my back while I worked.

Jill glanced at me again, and my abs flexed on their own. Swear to fucking God, I didn't do it on purpose.

"So, where you from?" I asked, needing to ease the tense energy rising between us before my dick's interest became too obvious.

"Here." She met my gaze, a stubborn hint in her eyes, red flushing her face.

"A few days ago, you said you were from out of town," I reminded her, although I wasn't bothered by her lie. People with secrets tended toward them. I would know. It'd been my words that had sent Alana away, and no one but Charley knew that.

Her gaze flitted away.

"You jog every morning?" I asked before she took off like a startled deer.

"Yep." She shoved her hands in her cutoff jean shorts pockets rather than wrap her arms around herself like she seemed to want to do.

"What else do you do for fun?" I screwed the cap back on my empty bottle.

"Work out, hike, read." She shrugged and glanced away.

"Go out to dinner with the Edwards."

"When they ask."

"And if *I* asked?" The question spilled without thought, jerking her focus back to my face. I held my breath, a heavy thump in my chest. Guess I'd made my choice about which someone I wanted to pursue—not that I really had a choice.

"I'm not looking to get involved, Kane," she finally answered, and my breath left in a rush.

"And I'm just a widowed man asking as a friend—if you want one. Figured with you being new to town and all and me ready to start living again..." I shrugged, not really sure how to finish the sentence or explain my draw to her. I didn't have words for it, but I wasn't going to push. I held her gaze, letting her see whatever she could read, whatever she hoped to see inside my eyes. I had nothing to hide.

"What about Charley?"

My brow twitched downward. "What about him?"

Jill watched me closely, but I didn't know what she hoped to figure out. No one else had—including the man who owned that part of me. She shrugged. "So, are you asking?"

"You to dinner?"

Pink flushed her cheeks again, and she nodded, glancing away, her teeth finding her lower lip.

"Guess I am," I said, a slow smile tilting my mouth.

That pink turned red, and she hunched her shoulders to hide her pebbled nipples. "Okay," she whispered.

"Really?" My quick, full-on grin matched the sudden lightness in my chest.

"Yeah." She glanced at me again. "But just friends, okay?"

"You got it." I tossed the empty water bottle into the back

of my truck and turned back to find her gaze glued to my abs.

"I gotta get back to work," she rushed to say but made no move to escape—or turn her gaze away from my abs.

"Tomorrow night?"

"Hmm?" She jerked her head up to look me in the face.

"Do you want to go to dinner with me tomorrow night?"

She bit down on her lower lip again, snagging my gaze. I imagined doing the nibbling, licking the plump flesh, tasting and breathing her in.

"Kane."

I raised an eyebrow and met her stare head-on, wondering at the lack of guilt. "Yeah?"

"Just friends."

My smirk happened without thought. "Yeah."

She nodded. "I'll go to dinner with you tomorrow night."

Just friends in words, but far from it in my mind.

A cooling breeze slid over my damp skin, and I blinked, waiting to hear Alana's thoughts on the wind, maybe even her blessing, but nothing whispered in my ears, same as always.

"Jenny's Place okay?" I asked Jill, focusing on the present. "There's isn't much else around here."

"Their burgers are the best. Just have to jog it off the next morning."

"I'll jog it off with ya," I offered, my smirk returning.

She eyed me for a few seconds. "I'd like that," she finally agreed, her voice soft, no trace of wariness in her eyes, but her chin lifted. "Annette assured me you're a good man, Kane Austin. If you prove her wrong, I'll kick your ass—friend or not."

I eyed her arms, far from masculine, but toned with definition. My mind went to her past since she didn't seem like a woman who liked to flex her muscles. "You look strong enough to," I told her.

She blinked, her chin and shoulders relaxing. "I *am* strong," she whispered, vulnerability in her eyes.

"You are," I agreed, hoping to give her the reassurance her whispered words seemed to suggest she needed. "Beautiful, too."

Wetness coated her chestnut-colored eyes.

"Friends can say that, right?" I asked, pulling my hammer from its hook on my tool belt.

She swallowed and nodded. "See you tomorrow night?" she asked, her voice a breathy whisper.

"Six?"

"Yeah, six." Her smile wobbled, and I nodded before forcing myself to turn away.

If she wanted to share her secrets, she would. Jill needed a friend, a shoulder to lean on. Anyone with half a brain could see that. Her being hot as hell might make being "just" friends hard—fucking pun intended—but I would be a man of my word until she decided otherwise.

If she decided otherwise.

Deciding to not question my lack of guilt, wanting to be more than a mere shoulder or worry about where things might lead with her, I went back to work, not quitting until it grew too dark to keep from smashing my thumb. Even then, I had energy to spare. Excitement, I forgot, tended to do that, even when one drank too much the night before.

Charley hadn't texted me the rest of the day, and even though I'd hoped he would, it was probably for the best. He could be my best friend, but I needed something else to fill my mind, and Jill did that easily. If only giving up thinking about Charley in my bed with the two of us came as easy.

'd thought Kane's serious face was heart-achingly beautiful, but seeing light in his eyes or a smirk on those full lips? Lordy, the man should have had a warning label attached to his chest. Going from closed off and antsy earlier that week to relaxed and flirting by the weekend... I guessed his healed friendship with Charley had turned his life around. He even came right out and said he was ready to start living again.

Happiness for both men swirled through me. I'd agreed to dinner with Kane, but I still found myself thinking about his friend. Both had visited me in my dreams the previous two nights—individually and at the same time.

I'd had no intention of dating anyone, let alone someone like Kane. Gorgeous, but far from cocky, add in kind, and those sweet tingles attacked every inch of my body. And *his* body? Like finely hewn marble with a sun-kissed golden tan. Every dip and valley rippling down his torso made my mouth water for a few licks.

He had no clue Charley wanted him, and even though I

really didn't want to hurt anyone, the temptation of Kane proved too much. I'd caved, even if it was as "just friends."

I stole a glance across the cab of his truck.

He'd covered those pecs and abs with a tight t-shirt, a mossy color that brought out the green in his eyes. Tension seemed to ride his shoulders as the windshield wipers swiped away the light falling rain. From the second I'd climbed into his truck and he shut the door behind me—a true gentleman—I'd noted his unease. The quietness in the cab annoyed me like a sock twisted inside my running shoes, and I couldn't deal.

"Are you okay?" I had to ask.

Kane flexed his fingers on the steering wheel and repositioned his hands as a slow, steady exhale lowered his shoulders. "It was storming the night my wife and daughter died."

Car accident, Annette had said. While it wasn't thunder and lightning overhead, the rain still splattered against the windshield of his truck.

"Do you want me to drive?" I asked quietly, studying his profile.

His lip curled slightly, but he shook his head. "I'm more nervous to be out with a 'just friend' than this little passing storm."

Just friends—what we agreed on, what I'd asked for. If Kane wasn't so damn sweet, soft-spoken, and kind, *and* if Annette hadn't taken every opportunity to sell the man to me, I wouldn't have thought about being more.

JD had been kind in the beginning, too, but there'd been hardness to him, jealousy whenever we'd gone out, and he caught other men looking at me. There'd been other red flags, but until a woman experiences them for herself, she usually doesn't take note until it's too late.

It'd been too late for me, but was it too late to maybe try again? Was I even ready to? Temptation warred with wariness—my body longed for more, but my head screamed, no. My gut told me Kane's genuine spirit would prove itself if given the chance.

"So, *friend*," I said, keeping my tone light, deciding to play things out and see where they went. "Tell me what you do for fun besides swing a hammer and enjoy the scent of sawdust."

"How do you know I like the scent of sawdust?"

I shrugged. "Who doesn't? Smells almost as good as being out in the middle of the woods after it rains."

He flitted his head my way. "You like the scent of sawdust?"

Smells like you, I almost blurted. *Delicious, like I can't draw you deep enough into my lungs.* Lips clamped shut, I opted for a nod. Charley smelled good, too, sandalwood and spice…

"You didn't answer my question," I reminded him, forcing thoughts of his friend from my mind.

"I make furniture and have a small woodshop beside my cabin."

"What kind?"

"All kinds. Bed frames, tables of all sorts, chairs."

"I'd love to see your work sometime. I've always been curious about working with your hands like that." Heat flushed through me at the thought of his *good* hands. "You know, having that instant gratification and all that."

Lordy, I needed to shut up.

"I can take you up to the shop after dinner if you want," Kane offered. "As just friends."

I let my smirk fly at his teasing tone. "I'd like that."

He glanced at me again, a twinkle in his eyes. "My turn?"

"For?"

"Asking questions."

My lips zippered shut again, and I focused on the mist still falling from the darkening sky.

"People around here like to pry, don't they?"

"Terribly so," I muttered, my arms finding their way around my middle, even though the seatbelt held me tight.

Kane laughed, the light sound easing my insides. "Well, if you plan on sticking around, better get used to it, especially living where you do."

"The Edwards are the sweetest couple I've ever met."

"They are."

"What do you know about them?" I asked, and Kane went with my topic change, filling me in on the gossip he knew—married for over sixty years, childless, and still lovebirds who spent two weeks in Aruba every December.

The sky cleared by the time we got to Jenny's Place, and my nerves kicked back into high gear after our easy conversation had lessened them.

Everyone knew everyone except for outsiders like me. It seemed I was the only one in the bar drawing attention.

People didn't bother to be covert, checking the two of us out, but at least most called a greeting to Kane. I expected we'd be the talk of the town for months to come—even if our "friendship" didn't last more than one date. I feigned smiles when he introduced me to a few of his old friends. We eventually made our way toward a table near the back.

Kane pulled out my chair for me and muttered a "Shit" while settling across from me with a heavy exhale.

"Are you alright?" I asked him, noting the unease creasing his brow.

"Yeah. Just feels weird being here with a woman." His smile didn't reach his eyes. "A *just friend*, woman."

My chuckle lightened his hazel eyes, easing hints of his smile in their depths. The *just* stuff was starting to get old. "Is it good to get out?"

"Yes," he didn't hesitate to answer. "You?" His stare bore into me, both of our smiles dissolving.

Back to the questions we go.

The waitress kept me from having to answer, thank God, but Kane crossed his arms and leaned onto the table the second she walked off with our order for burgers and soda.

"What are you doing up here in bum-fuck no-man's-land, Jill? Those jeans you wear aren't off a Walmart or second-hand store's rack, and that subtle perfume, making my mouth water, couldn't have come cheap."

Damnit.

Unable to escape the intensity in his eyes, I turned away, my stomach clenching even as dampness coated my panties. *His mouth watered*—he wanted to taste me as much as my tongue salivated to lick along those muscles, I got more than an eye full of the day before.

"Annette says you have secrets."

My gaze jerked back toward him.

He stared, waiting.

I stared—until a shiver licked down my spine and pulled my focus off his stormy eyes toward Jenny's entrance.

Charley stood in the doorway, his gaze flitting between me and his friend, his slow smile easing the anxiety Kane had stirred up with his questions but rousing a double portion of butterflies in its place.

"Charley," Kane muttered, but I couldn't make out his tone. Disappointment? Longing?

I turned back to find his attention settled on his friend, his eyes betraying every thought in his head—definitely longing, almost a primal need. "We all have secrets, don't we, Kane?"

He blinked, his brow furrowed as the emotion in his troubled gaze shuttered off.

Charley's sudden presence beside our table stole the air from between us, our lips parting at the same time, solidifying in my mind the fact we both felt drawn to him. Kane turned toward his friend first, his smile so damn forced, Charley must have noticed.

"Charley."

"Good to see you out, Kane." His low voice pebbled my skin, nipples included.

I glanced up to find Charley smiling, no trace of jealousy in his tone or etched into his face, even though I sat with the man whose ass he craved. No jealousy? Did he love Kane that much, he wanted his happiness, no matter the cost to his own heart? My own swooned at the thought—two good men who turned me into a tingly, wet mess.

Charley's gaze slid to me, settling on my lips briefly before flitting up to my eyes. "Jill."

"Charley." *Breathless as a whore. Lovely.*

He flashed a grin before turning back toward Kane. "Can't blame you, man."

Kane's shoulders relaxed, and he sat back, hands on his thighs. "You don't mind?"

"Why would I?"

Glancing between the two men, I shifted on my seat, more from embarrassment than the arousal coursing through me. The floor called to me, promising to suck me beneath its wooden planks if I wished. I opened my mouth to excuse myself to the bathroom to escape, but Charley's gaze returned to me, catching my voice before it reached my lips.

"Kane's a good man."

"So, Annette says," I spewed the first thing to come to mind.

Charley chuckled. "What's she say about me?"

That you moped without him in your life. That you used to peer up the mountain as though hoping to catch a glimpse of him. I can only imagine the longing in your heart, your body, yet you're willing to give him up...

"Nothing," I lied.

"Huh." He grunted, his eyes narrowing. "Annette doesn't say *nothing* about anyone."

"What has she said about me?" I tossed back, surprised by my own sass, but afraid of what the answer might be.

Charley's grin turned downright sinful, and my pussy ached with a need I'd never felt before. "Said she'll skin me alive if I hurt you."

"Good thing I'm at dinner with Kane, then, isn't it?" I said, a smile flirting on my lips as my heart thundered in my chest.

He chuckled again. "You're a lucky bastard, Kane."

"We're just friends," Kane muttered as though disappointed.

I was starting to regret those words.

Charley offered me a wink and moved off, more of a saunter than I'd seen from him on Friday night. My gaze tracked after him long enough, I cleared my throat while turning back to my just friend date.

Kane stared at his hands, his brow furrowed.

I chewed on my lower lip.

He hadn't acted jealous over Charley's words—but he also claimed to just want to be friends.

I'm on a date with Kane and lusting after Charley.

My insides stilled like the calm before a storm. JD's voice whispered in my head, curling my shoulders inward.

Cheating whore. Worthless bitch.

Kane lifted his focus, not his head, peering at me through dark lashes as though sensing the sudden shift inside me. "Jill?"

I swallowed and attempted a smile. "I-I'm okay."

He glanced over at Charley, who slid onto a stool at the bar. "You like him."

It wasn't an accusation, more a simple acknowledgment, but my stomach churned. Lifting my chin, I was tempted to echo his words back to him. "He's a good-looking man," I said instead, hating that my tone sounded defensive as hell. I'd grown a tiny set of balls since leaving JD.

"He's single." Kane met my gaze again, heating my cheeks with the question in his tone.

"Are you trying to talk me into wanting your friend?"

"Maybe." He shrugged and glanced at Charley's back as he sat beside the guy Annette had wanted to hook me up with on Friday night.

The waitress returned with our food, and I turned my attention to the need for sustenance, although I'd lost all desire for food.

Did he want me? Didn't he want me? Why tell me Charley was available?

Damnit, my stomach twisted. Catching Charley watching the two of us over his shoulder, his face unreadable didn't help matters *at all*.

What the hell have I gotten myself into?

I told myself I would step back and give Kane up because I loved him, but seeing him sit with Jill, his focus on her even as hers flitted my way, hurt like hell. I'd given him up once before, and faced with actually doing it again, hurt almost as much as losing him the first time to my sister.

Instead of ordering the burger and onion rings I'd come to Jenny's for, I opted for a single beer and nursed the shit out of it, blowing off everyone who tried to talk to me, including the long-winded fucker beside me. Eventually, he left me the hell alone, and I stewed in self-pity. I fucking allowed myself that moment—that hour—rather than suck it up and be a man.

Nothing wrong with having feelings, I just didn't need to show them to the rest of the goddamn world.

It wasn't just losing Kane again that stung, though. Jealousy over his sitting with Jill knifed as well. Hell, I was jealous of them *both*. I knew she was interested in me, but I wouldn't fuck up Kane's chance at finding happiness again.

"How's your dad, Charley?" Jenny's granddaughter, Tess, refilled the beer pretzel bowl beside me.

Since I couldn't be an asshole to the woman whose place where I enjoyed hanging out, I forced a smile. "Not good. Surprised he's still alive."

Lips pursed, she shook her head. "Miss him around here."

He was a strict, religious man who enjoyed his beer. Never did understand how he could judge others about splinters while ignoring the own plank in his eye—or however that Bible verse went. Tess missed him. Call me a heartless bastard, but I sure as fuck wouldn't when the good Lord called his ass home.

He refused help from me or anyone and refused to let me put him in the assisted living house closer to Renovo to make the rest of his life easier. He wanted to die like a man, in his own home, in his own bed, he'd shared with Mom for forty years. Stubborn bastard.

Every day I got home, I expected to find him laid out on his bed, his soul finally with Mom, his body mine to deal with. He'd been a good provider for his family—I wouldn't steal that legacy from him—but love? He'd only had enough for Mom and Alana.

I'd accepted that fact years earlier, even found a sense of appreciation since I'd learned to stand on my own, find my own inner strength. He didn't have softness to spare, but I never went without, thanks to Mom and my twin. Admitting I loved my best friend would have gotten me kicked out on my ass at age eighteen unless I got myself "right" with God and repented for my sins.

As if love could possibly be a sin. Dad didn't know the first goddamn thing about it.

I could feel it deep in my soul like an all-consuming fire. I could *feel* Kane behind me like some paranormal mojo linked us together. But awareness of Jill radiated along with that energy I'd known since the fifth grade.

I finished off my beer and stood, feeling both of their gazes as I pulled a twenty from my pocket. Tossing it on the bar, I glanced their way.

Yep, they both watched me, but Jill's gaze flitted to Kane the second I made eye contact with her. I turned away, torn and fucking confused as hell. "Have a good one, Tess," I called out, and she smiled and waved.

"Give your dad my love!"

Wouldn't be doing that, but I nodded and waved.

Jenny's door slammed shut behind me, and I stood in the dimly lit parking lot, filling my lungs with the cool night air. Muffled voices and music reached me through the door, but the shrill of night insects drew me away from the sounds of civilization.

The earlier rain shower pulled in cooler air, and I hitched my shoulders while stalking across the dirt-packed parking lot. My truck sat at the edge of the lot, and I climbed in, ready to call it quits for the night. I stayed put, though, my heartbeat loud in my ears, watching Jenny's door. Waiting, but for what, exactly, I didn't know.

I wanted Kane but wanted Jill, too.

It wasn't my place to suggest fucking, that would have to be Kane's for a change. Hell knew, he obviously felt guilty as fuck, out with another woman than Alana, but he shouldn't.

Every time the door opened, my heart rate kicked up, but a full twenty minutes passed before Jill and Kane exited. Neither glanced my way in the dark corner opposite his truck. He opened the passenger door and shut her in while I stared, damn jealousy eating my gut.

Kane rounded his truck and climbed in. Seconds later, they drove off, and I turned my key, pulling out slowly behind them. Knowing he had to drop her off at the Edwards, I hung back far enough, I lost sight every couple of seconds as they rounded a bend, following along the meandering river.

I told myself to turn around and go home. I told myself I didn't want to know if he dropped her off or drove up the mountain to his cabin deep in the woods. I couldn't turn, though. Clenching my goddamn steering wheel, I followed like a perverted prick, my gut a rock, my dick just as hard. Kane slowed but didn't turn into the Edwards. He kept right on past, his tires taking him onto his dirt driveway beyond.

Ten years earlier, I'd have followed him, uninvited or not. He'd have let me in, and we'd have talked our way into whatever woman he had in his clutches. He'd been a smooth talker once upon a time. Did he still have it? Did he plan on moving on with his life like I'd encouraged him? It sure as fuck seemed that way—but I'd given him the go-ahead, indirectly told him I didn't mind his moving on from Alana. If only I had the balls to tell him I minded his moving on from *me*.

"Fuck." I slowed, passing his driveway, his taillights disappearing around a switchback.

Ten years ago, Kane wouldn't have minded.

But now?

I felt I didn't know the man he'd become. I didn't know what he needed or what he wanted. Sure, he spilled his guts and seemed to want to move on, but guilt had gnawed at him when he'd seen me walk into Jenny's.

Blowing a breath past my lips, I told myself I needed to let him go. Needed to let him heal. Maybe someday, things could go back to the way they were, but fuck, it hurt like hell to drive away.

"All of it?" Jill stood inside my front door, her gaze scanning my small cabin.

"All but the couch cushions, yeah."

"Unbelievable."

"I've never brought anyone up here," I told her as she moved closer to inspect the couch I'd built.

"Really?"

"Yeah."

"How long have you lived up here?" She eyed the coffee table with its lacquered finish.

"Five years." I considered hanging up my keys on the hook beside the door but wasn't sure what either of our intentions was. The thought of more twitched my dick, but I forced thoughts of sex from my mind—unsure I was ready for that mentally, even though my body sure as hell was. "Bought the land and lived in a tent while building it."

"You're brave." She turned and smiled at me, rubbing her palms down her jeans. "Aren't there bears up here? Big cats?"

"Haven't seen any, but yeah, they're around."

"I'm always afraid of running into one while jogging."

"Carry a bottle of mace."

"I always do."

One of my eyebrows hiked up. "Got it on you now?"

"Of course." She fished a small canister from her back pocket.

"Then I best not jump you, huh?" I asked with a glint in my eye. "How about a drink instead?"

"Sure." Her smile didn't appear forced as she put the mace away.

I left my post by the front door and grabbed a couple of beers from the fridge, the damn butterflies in my stomach, making my hands a little shaky.

Jill sat on the couch, her gaze roaming over everything but me.

I sat beside her and handed her a bottle. "Cheers to finding new friends."

She nibbled her lower lip, smiling and clinking her bottle against mine. "You ought to be selling this stuff," she said after a small swig. "Do you have a website?"

"No."

"Why not?"

"It's just a hobby. Made a hutch for Annette and Roy, and a rocking chair for my mom." I shrugged and lifted my beer to my lips. "A few other pieces, but nothing serious."

"You made that hutch?"

I nodded and swallowed the cold brew.

"Wow." Jill studied my face. "Seriously, Kane, you could do well for yourself making furniture. You're very talented."

"What does a city girl know about woodworking?"

She glanced away quick as fuck.

I'd hit a nerve.

"Enough," she whispered.

We drank in silence as tension rose, but more than just discomfort from questions. The sweet yet spicy scent of her subtle perfume kept wafting past my nose every time she moved. Her plump lips parted and touched the beer bottle, a flick of her tongue catching the drip left behind. The pulse in her neck thrummed, the quick rise and fall of her chest and its hardened points sending the blood straight to my dick.

"Are you on social media at all?" she asked, her voice rushed. "Setting up a page or a website is free. I could help you do it."

"I prefer to live a quiet life."

Jill studied her hands wrapped around her beer. "Kind of hard to do around here with everyone knowing everyone."

"Imagine the gossip after tonight."

"Ugh." She grimaced. "I can imagine. Annette is going to grill me for all the details of our date."

"Date? I thought we were just two friends, hanging out." Yeah, I totally went there, probing, fishing.

She finally lifted her head, her gaze landing on my lips.

Fuck, I wanted to make a move, especially when her tongue flitted out again to wet her lower lip. I imagined Charley on the chair across from his, stroking his dick through his jeans, watching us.

"Friends can kiss, right?" I rasped out, the need to feel her lips on mine like a sudden punch to my gut.

She made no move to answer but blinked and lifted her gaze to mine. Pupils blown wide seemed answer enough.

I leaned closer, slow enough she could back away or send

her fist into my nose if she wanted. Pausing a mere foot away from her face, my body tight as fuck, I held still. "Jill?"

"Yeah, Kane?" Her breathless tone jerked my dick in its prison, and I clenched my jaw against the groan wanting to rumble my chest.

"Can I kiss you?"

"Ye—"

I closed the distance, cutting her off.

Fuck.

Soft, pliant, and so damn feminine and sweet.

I stroked my tongue along her lower lip, and she opened, letting me in. My free hand tangled in her hair. She tasted of hops, the satiny feel of her tongue against mine, the plump cushion of her lips ripping every thought but *Jill* from my damn brain.

She whimpered, and I eased back, unsure of the sound. Eyes huge, she stared at me, lips parted, the pulse in her neck, pounding in time with the one in my ears.

"You okay?" My voice sounded like a goddamn croaking frog.

She rubbed her lips together and nodded.

I wanted to dive back in and take with force, not gentleness. It fucking hurt to hold back.

Been so fucking long...

"Too much, too soon?" she asked, her voice quiet and eyes concerned, and I realized I frowned. "I'm sorry. I didn't mean to make you feel guilty."

I let out a heavy exhale and backed out of her personal space, every cell in my body vibrating to move forward, to touch and claim. "You didn't." I huffed a wry laugh as the truth of my frown settled into my consciousness. "Actually, I wasn't even thinking about Alana. I feel guiltier over *that* than kissing you."

Jill continued to study me. "Don't force yourself if you aren't ready, Kane."

"Shouldn't you be more worried about me using you to help me move on?"

"You're not that kind of man."

I held her gaze. "You don't know me."

"I trust Annette."

Yeah, but I didn't trust myself.

"What's on your mind, Kane?"

I touched the lock of dark hair hanging over her shoulder, wishing to thread my fingers through it and tug while brushing my knuckles over her breast. "Taking you back to my bed."

Red fused through her cheeks, and I pulled away again, lifting the bottle I still clutched in my hand to finish off the beer.

"You're so damn pretty, Jill." I cast a quick glance at her wide eyes and the desire luring me in like a juicy worm on a hook. "I'll take you down the mountain before I push things too far."

She hesitated long enough. I thought she wanted me to take her to my bed. "Okay."

Nodding, I stood and adjusted myself as discretely as possible. "Come on."

She took my offered hand, and part of my insides shifted, seeming to slide into place.

But Charley's chair sat empty, and my chest ached.

Kane went jogging with me Monday morning as the sky began to lighten. No questions, just companionable silence as our feet slapped the blacktop, and birds chirped their welcome to the sun.

At the halfway point up Warren's Run, I slowed and veered off the road, taking a small path I'd found a few days earlier that led into the cold mountain water gurgling in the distance. Huge rocks scattered through the swishing stream, and I knelt beside it to drink my fill.

"Definitely not a city girl if you're drinking like that," Kane said with a laugh. He knelt beside me to drink, and I hopped atop the closest rock for a little rest.

Kane settled beside me, and I breathed deeply as my lungs relaxed, the clean air scented with soil and old forest leaves filling my lungs. Hints of Kane's soap wafted past, warming me in places the jogging hadn't.

"So quiet," I whispered. "Best place to meditate."

"You come here every day?"

"If my head needs to be cleared or I need to work something out."

We sat a few minutes, listening to the trickling water and chirping birds flitting around us. His presence, while still tingling my body with awareness, no longer set me on edge. He'd kept his hands to himself the night before, not taking advantage of having me alone deep in the woods, far from where anyone might hear me scream for help.

JD had taken advantage of me the second he'd been afforded the chance. I hadn't minded at the time.

I didn't think I would have minded if Kane had pushed for more the night before, but I appreciated his restraint. Lordy knew, his body had given his self-control a run for its money. He'd stood and offered his hand, and I'd caught an eyeful of the thick ridge inside his jeans.

The memory of it rushed those tingles straight between my thighs, and I squeezed my inner walls tight, wishing for so much more than friendship.

I exhaled a heavy breath, my feet getting itchy to run. "Ready?"

Kane eyed my lips, a slight smirk on his. "For tasting your lips again?"

Heat rushed through me, staining my cheeks, and I let out a light laugh.

"I'm ready to run if that's what you're suggesting," he said, a twinkle in his eyes.

Shaking, I pushed to my feet and hopped off the rock. "You can kiss me—if you can catch me." I took off like a rabbit, loping up the trail.

The sound of his footfalls rose behind me, and I laughed,

slowing on purpose. He grasped my elbow and swung me around, into his arms.

"Caught ya."

Kane swallowed my laughter with his mouth, and I melted against his hard chest, drinking him in, breathing him in, until the woods disappeared in a buzzing background. The lumberjack could kiss. Hell, better than any man I'd tasted. Soft, supple lips for a man, but he moved them with purpose and strength, trailing along my jaw after releasing my mouth and weakening my knees with the brush of his whiskers on my sensitive skin.

"Race you back to the store," he whispered against my ear, pebbling my entire body with goosebumps.

"What do I get if I win?" I asked, a breathless, wonton woman in need of the hard-on brushing my thigh.

"Another dinner date."

"As just friends?"

Kane pulled back, all trace of jollity gone from his face. "No."

Luscious shivers rippled through me. "And if you win?"

"I'll think of something."

Lordy, the suggestion in his voice…

He released me and took off, his sneakers flipping dead pine needles up in the air behind his heels.

Laughing, my stomach erupting with butterflies, I took off after him, making sure to let him reach the store first.

"So, what's your prize for winning?" I asked, hunched over and sucking wind, hands on my knees while eyeing his ass as he bent, doing the same.

"I'll think of something," he repeated in the same suggestive tone.

I felt Annette's eyes on us but didn't glance at the store. She would grill me for the details, but Kane left for work without giving me any goods to fuel her gossiping.

He stopped for coffee Tuesday and Wednesday, and I made sure to be around the store when I knew he headed to work. Thursday, he asked me to dinner for Friday night in front of Annette, who sat on her plastic chair, pretending to read a tattered novel, a smile firmly fixed on her face. Her smile widened when I agreed, and we exchanged numbers.

I caught myself staring at his lips whenever he came into the store, remembering the taste of him, the sweetness of his breath. Warmth tingled to life between my thighs every time my gaze landed on him. The downtrodden look on his face the first time I'd met him hadn't returned. His eyes twinkled with life, and warmth filled me to think I might have helped him move on.

But how far did I want to help? What were his true intentions?

While Annette sang his praises, the jaded part of me insisted I keep up walls. Don't trust any man, especially since he seemed too good to be true.

Then there was the Charley factor. I couldn't get that man out of my mind, even though we'd only seen each other twice and briefly at that.

He pulled into the parking lot on Friday morning while I planted snap peas along the stick and twine fence I'd built for their vines.

I glanced up to find him hot as hell in his dark green uniform as he climbed from a truck with "Game Warden" written along its side. The pants hugged his thighs, and the sight of the holster and belt around his trim waist did funny things to my insides.

I didn't like lawmen, but Charley looked damn fine with his sharp, shaved jaw and rigid set to his wide shoulders.

My heart tripped in its beating.

He approached me, and although I couldn't make out his eyes in the distance, I felt the intensity of his stare. I stood on shaking legs and brushed the dirt from my knees without taking my focus off his steady gait.

"Good morning, Jill."

Lordy, that rumbling tone. My smile wobbled. "Morning."

He glanced around the garden that hadn't yet sprouted a shoot. "Roy keeping you busy?"

"This is my newfound hobby."

"I can imagine you get bored around here," he said, returning his attention to me.

"Not really." I shoved my hands in my pockets to keep them from trembling. Weakness still plagued my knees, and my heart continued to pound in my chest. Swallowing against the sudden dryness in my mouth, I glanced away from his intense stare.

"Did you have a good night out with Kane?"

Heat flushed through me, and I shuffled my feet. "Yes. Have you seen his place?" I asked, needing to end the questions.

"I have."

"He's amazingly talented." I thought of his hands and went to a boiling point in a flash. "With wood." *Oh God.* "Working," I hastened to add. "Woodworking, making furniture." I rubbed my lips together, desperate to calm my racing heart. Damnit, Charley Woodhill got my head in a tizzy.

"I don't harbor any bad feelings toward you, Jill. Quite the opposite."

I jerked my gaze back toward him.

"Alana is gone, and I want Kane to be happy."

Chewing on the inside of my lip, I considered his words. "You love him, don't you?"

A frown flitted over his stoic face but disappeared just as quickly. "Like a brother."

He lied, but it wasn't my place to call him out. I didn't know him well enough, and it wasn't my damn business, anyway. But the pain in his eyes, perhaps regret, made me want to make things right, give both of them their own happily ever after.

"He loves you," I voiced what anyone with eyes could see.

Charley glanced away but made no other move to solidify the unease his eyes revealed. "I just want him to be happy."

"And I want you both to be happy."

That intense stare returned to my face. "You don't even know me."

I shrugged, no clue how to explain what I felt for him … for Kane. Lordy, for the *two* of them and how they both made my insides twist and yearn for something I shouldn't. "I'd like to."

"Have dinner with me tomorrow night."

It wasn't a request, and I didn't do well with commands, but Charley's eyes softened rather than hardening like JD's did whenever he barked at me to do something.

"I can't."

"Can't or don't want to?" His gaze probed straight through me, and I knew there would be no hiding from Charley, an alpha to Kane's seemingly beta nature.

My pussy pulsed, and I shoved against thoughts of them together. I seriously needed to ease up on the male-on-male romance I'd found a sudden hunger for. My poor e-reader had been drained of its battery every night since I'd seen the two of them together. The batteries in my vibrator got the same workout.

Face surely red as a damn rose, I realized I hadn't yet answered. "I-I have plans."

"Some other time, then?"

Would Kane be upset if I went out for dinner with Charley? We had no understanding beyond going out for a real date the following night, but I also didn't want to hurt anyone.

"I'm going out with Kane," I blurted.

He nodded. "Figured as much." Disappointment filled his eyes, and I realized I'd hurt him with my words.

"We're just friends."

A low chuckle left him, but the laughter didn't light his eyes. "No woman is just friends with Kane Austin."

I wondered about him, wanting to be more than just friends. Ugh, what a mess. "I'd be better off avoiding both of you," I muttered my thought out loud.

"Want to eat the cake, too?" His eyebrow quirked upward, and arousal, slick and wet, rose inside me. His gaze suggested a hell of a lot more than I knew how to handle. That dark gaze of his slid down to my lips and stayed there.

Have your cake and eat it, too.

Yes, please.

My heartbeat thrummed in my ears. What was I going to do?

"So, back to my question."

"Which one?" I whispered, still thinking about two slices of cake with sugary sweet frosting my taste buds drooled for.

"Some other time," Charley said. "Dinner."

"I'd like that." I damn well meant it. Perhaps my "real" date with Kane would give me some clarity on the situation. If it didn't, I would outright ask Kane if he minded.

Or you could just invite Charley along.

KANE TEXTED ME FRIDAY AFTERNOON, telling me he'd picked up a couple steaks from the store on his way home. Did I want to dine in? His place?

My hands shook as I texted back, agreeing to head up the mountain at six-thirty.

Annette winked and told me to have a good time. "He's a catch, that one," she said as I shoved my cell back in my pocket. "A good man."

But a worthless whore didn't deserve a good man.

JD's words crashed in my head while I readied for my dinner date with Kane, and I chanted the words I needed to settle my head.

I am strong.

I am beautiful.

My affirmations didn't convince me, especially as my heart played tug of war between two faces, two men in love with each other, who thought they hid their feelings.

I didn't even get my car into park when Kane pulled open his cabin door, a grin on his face.

"Hey, beautiful," he called, his gaze sliding over the

sundress I'd opted for since the warmth returned to the mountains.

Beautiful.

"Charley asked me out," I blurted even as Kane's words warmed me through.

His smile faltered, but he held it in place as I walked toward him.

"I'm sorry," I rushed to say, hating whatever pain I'd inflicted. "I don't want to come between the two of you. I didn't even know what to say to him, what you would think."

"What *did* you say?"

I stood before Kane, tilting back my head since he stood atop the granite stairs leading to his front door. Guilt over wanting to get to know Charley swooped in and choked the breath out of me.

"He's a good-looking man," Kane murmured.

I clutched the pie I'd brought a little closer to my twisting stomach. "He is."

"So, when are you two going out?"

"I didn't agree to anything specific."

"Because you wanted to check with me first?" He studied my face, his own gaze as intense as Charley's had been earlier. Perhaps Kane wasn't all beta as I'd originally thought. My heart pounded so harshly, I couldn't seem to catch my breath.

"Yes?"

"I have no claim over you, Jill." Kane's tone and eyes softened. "You're free to do whatever you want."

A swift exhale sagged my shoulders. "I want to have dinner with you."

His lips twitched. "Then come on in."

Hardly settled but feeling a tiny bit better—even without a real answer of what he thought about my going out with Charley—I did as Kane said.

He grilled one hell of a steak, baked the perfect potato, and even had sour cream and fresh chives for on top.

Neither of us brought up the topic of Charley, the damn elephant that needed addressing.

I'd brought the strawberry rhubarb pie Roy had shown me how to bake that morning, and listening to Kane groan around the first bite of our dessert had those non-stop tingles between my thighs, begging for release.

"Do you lift weights?" he asked, forking up another bite.

His question knocked my brain for a loop for a few seconds. "Huh?"

"Your arms. You're buff as hell for a woman."

"Oh." I glanced down at my bare arms and back up at him. "I used to before moving up here."

"So, you're *not* from around here."

I pressed my lips tight. Lying when he'd been nothing but open and honest with his feelings—at least to me—filled me with shame. "I'm starting over, Kane."

He nodded and went back to his pie, seemingly content with my explanation.

"Are muscular arms on a woman a turn off?" I asked, needing to take our conversation away from where JD's words would whisper in my head.

"Not at all."

Considering, I thought he had a hard-on for his best friend with the wide shoulders and muscles bulging beneath shirts, his answer didn't surprise me.

"So, why lift weights?" he asked before I thought of what to say next.

"Why all the questions?" I shot back even though my hackles didn't rise.

"Because I want to know you." He shoved another forkful of pie in his mouth and held my gaze while chewing.

I stared, my thoughts in a whirl. "What is this, Kane? What are we doing?" Hell knew, I had no clue. Between wanting Kane and Charley and trying to remind myself I'd sworn off men … my head spun.

"This is me interested in you. You interested in me."

"And if I accept Charley's offer of dinner?" I spewed.

There. Elephant addressed. I held my breath.

"Then it's you interested in him, too." No trace of jealousy or anger flinched his face.

"So, you wouldn't mind if I went out with your best friend after having dinner with you?" I asked, surprised by his lack of annoyance at either Charley or me.

"Not at all."

I chewed on a small bite of pie, considering the sincerity in his tone. Temptation to ask if he wanted to tag along rose, but...

"What do *you* want, Jill?"

"I-I don't know." Honestly, I didn't. "What about you?" I asked, no more than a mere whisper.

"I want you." No question in that statement or the look in his eyes.

My breath caught, and instant need flared through my body.

"Stay the night with me, Jill."

"Kane..." I swallowed against the tightness in my throat, even as arousal slickened between my thighs.

He leaned on the small table, getting as close as he could to peer into my eyes. "I'm not asking to own you," he whispered, empathy and all the feels in his eyes. "I just want to hold you."

Temptation, hot and heavy, swung its blade at my jaded heart.

How did he know? Had I said too much? Did he already know how much I longed for the very thing he did?

I trusted Kane. Trusted the open vulnerability in his gaze, his manners, his gentleness when kissing me. I didn't deserve such a good man, but I found myself wanting to be worthy.

"I'm damn tired of being lonely," he rasped.

I didn't overthink his words or take offense, he might want to use me for his own selfish reasons. Lonely was a word I understood all too well. Even when married to JD, I'd experienced the type of aloneness that ate away at one's soul. Hell, I'd been lonely since my parents had passed.

"I'll stay," I agreed quietly, my heart in my throat.

An hour later, Kane flicked off his bedroom light, and I strained to make out his shadow in the dark as he undressed. My pulse thrummed. My lips tingled.

He crawled onto his bed behind me, gently pulling me back against his bare chest. One of his t-shirts acted as my nightie, but the heat of his skin burned through the thin cotton. He kept his groin away from my ass and his hands on my belly.

My heart pounded, and I fought for calm, waiting for him to push for more.

He didn't. His hot breath wafted over my neck as he let out a contented sigh, settling silence over us.

My heart ached, knowing I'd made him happy.

But what about Charley?

Kane's breathing evened out in sleep long before I drifted off.

CHARLEY

*D*ad didn't come down for breakfast when I called. When I didn't hear him getting ready for church by his usual time, I went up to check on the old bastard, poking my head into his and Mom's bedroom.

He laid peaceful and pale on his bed—too pale.

I pushed in the door. "Dad?"

No answer, not a twitch of muscle, indicated he'd heard me. No pulse struggled beneath my fingertips held against his cool neck.

"Give them all my love, Dad," I whispered before heading off to find my cell.

I LAID the last of my immediate family to rest on Thursday beneath gray skies. A handful of people showed—our neighbors and Kane, although they'd arrived separately. It was good to see them talking quietly after Dad's pastor said a few words over the casket.

Jill came with the Edwards, her quiet words of condolence as comforting as Kane's.

While I hadn't expected to grieve for the man, a deep sense of sadness sat on my shoulders. I knew he was finally at peace. His passing left me free from responsibility for another person, even though complete loneliness awaited me back home. He'd been a bastard, but the noises of him in the house, the quiet conversations we shared over what we could agree on, had filled the silence.

My gaze tracked Jill and Kane, and I smiled at Jill as she glanced over her shoulder at me before following the Edwards to their car.

Tess gave me a hard hug, and I wished I found the little blonde attractive. Two years older, still single ... maybe Jenny's granddaughter and I could have had a companionable relationship, my heart belonged to Kane.

The first spattering of light rain fell as I turned away from Dad's grave.

Kane waited by his truck parked next to mine. He'd started his life over, and I suddenly found myself feeling left behind.

A few guys from work had shown for the burial, and I took time to clasp hands and nod thanks over their words offering support. I wanted nothing more than to escape them and get to the man who continued to wait as the rain fell. Shoulders hunched, I made my way toward him.

"Thanks for coming," I told him.

He nodded, his gaze probing.

I shut down my hurt, my need for comfort. "Your parents seemed happy to finally see your ass."

"Yeah." He pushed off his truck and glanced up at the

cloudy sky, spitting down on us. "Been staying away too much." He seemed to sense my desire to leave Dad's death behind. Fuck knew, Kane had heard and seen enough of my childhood home life to know no love had existed between my father and me.

"Never too late to make a change," I said, wishing I'd had a close relationship with my parents like he had. Ready for a topic change, I cleared my throat. "How are things going with Jill?"

"Good."

"You fuck her yet?"

"No."

I let out a quiet exhale, lowering my shoulders and easing the tension in my gut. "Taking things slow or don't want to?"

"Not sure she's ready."

"Are you?" I held my damn breath.

"I miss that bond of connection, yeah."

I slapped his back, intending to joke about connection, but he pulled me in for a real hug—tight. Closing my eyes, I gave in to the need to melt, to be vulnerable. My throat tightened as I clung to him. He smelled like wood smoke and the same damn soap I'd secretly sniffed on him when we'd been teens. The twitch in my dick had me stepping back.

"Thanks." My voice hinted at my grief instead of lust, thank fuck.

Kane squeezed my shoulder, and I allowed myself to get lost in his eyes. "Call me if you need me."

I nodded, unable to speak.

He climbed into his truck, and I did the same—alone and empty.

I took Friday off because it was expected. Before dinner, I had all of Dad's shit packed up and ready for the Goodwill store. Temptation to call Kane to meet me for drinks had me fiddling with my cell, but fear of his being out with Jill kept me from calling. The same fear kept me from heading to Jenny's on my own.

The weekend loomed ahead since I didn't work until Monday. Knowing Kane was working for the Edwards on Saturday, I decided to head up that way in the morning and see if he needed help.

Kane grinned when I pulled my truck alongside his. "You here to work or watch?" he called when I hopped out of my truck.

I shook his hand and went in for a bro hug, sucking in a lungful of sweaty Kane while I could. "I'll give you a hand."

His eyes glinted.

"Fucker," I muttered, turning away so he wouldn't see the heat I couldn't keep from rising to my face.

Kane chuckled, and I cast a quick glance around. No Jill.

"You doing okay?" he asked.

"Yeah. Been readying myself for this for months, expected it, but still. Just didn't expect to hate the damn quiet at home."

"I know the feeling."

Shit. Why the fuck couldn't I just open my damn mouth and tell him we didn't have to be alone or lonely? Why the fuck couldn't I make myself vulnerable?

A pile of plywood sat, ready to cover the skeleton he'd raised on the cabin's concrete slab.

"You measure, I'll cut," I told him, heading to the table saw he'd set up.

We hung half the cabin's walls before I found my balls. "You go out last night?"

"Went down to that rib's joint in Lock Haven for something different."

I hit the power button and ripped down a piece of plywood to finish up the side we hung, working through my feelings. "A real night out on the town, huh?"

"Didn't feel like giving the locals something more to gossip about," he muttered when I handed him the sheet.

"Too late." I chuckled and swiped beads of sweat off my forehead. "Even your mom has you married off to the new girl in town."

"Not damn near ready for that again."

I wasn't ready for him to move on that much again, either. "Jill seems like a nice girl."

"Nice enough, she caught your eye, too. Heard you asked her out."

"I did."

"Want me to step back?" Kane asked. "Because I will if she's what you've been waiting for."

Well, fuck.

I opened my mouth to spew it all, to ask him if he loved me in the same way I did him, but Jill's apartment door opened, jerking my focus from his face and stealing my words, my thoughts—cut off jean shorts, legs for miles, a tight tank hugging her tits and small waist, two bottles of water in her hands, and a smile like sunshine.

"Fine as fuck, isn't she?"

I cleared my throat and turned away, grabbing another

piece of plywood. Fate had intervened to keep me from admitting my feelings for Kane. I told myself I was thankful I didn't end up making a fool of myself. He might want me happy, but he wouldn't love me, even if he didn't blame me for Alana and Nat's deaths.

I felt Jill approach, my body's awareness, raising the hairs on my arms.

"You guys thirsty?"

If only she knew how much—for both her and Kane.

My body torn in two directions, I turned. Pink fused her cheeks, and she quickly glanced away when I reached for the water, she held out. I guzzled it down, my gaze glued to her. Kane's stare heated the side of my face, but I couldn't look away from her.

She shoved her hands in her pockets, slouching her shoulders, the air of vulnerability about her tugging on my protective nature. Kane's character was the same in that way. It was no wonder she drew us both in so easily.

I wanted to know what made Jill want to curl in on herself and look at the ground as though she wanted it to swallow her whole. Her body language screamed insecurity, and I wanted to wrap her in my arms and tell her whatever she needed to hear. If only I knew what that was.

"Thanks for the water," I said, the first lame thing that popped into my head.

"You two looked hot down here in the sun."

"Hot, huh?" Kane joked. Leave it to him to make her smile while I made her nervous.

"Ha ha," she tossed his way, deadpan, but eyes twinkling.

"It wasn't the sawdust you really came down here for?" he asked her, his tone still light.

She glanced up at him through her lashes with the kind of smirk that would stiffen any man's dick.

Yep. No fucking doubt she wanted him, but goddamnit, so did I. Fuck it. I wasn't waiting. "Jill."

She glanced at me.

"Got plans for tonight?"

A quick lick over her lower lip with her pink tongue and she glanced back at Kane, either afraid he might get jealous or asking his permission.

"I was thinking the two of you could come over to my place tonight for a couple drinks," I added before either spoke. I felt Kane's stare—he knew where I was going, but it was Jill's widening pupils that held my attention.

I might fuck things up for Kane, but with Dad's death, the complete loneliness at home brought on a desperate feeling I'd never experienced before. For the first time, I didn't want to be the one stepping back. But I also wanted them both. Too much to hope for, but…

"I don't have plans," Jill said, glancing at Kane again.

I turned toward my best friend—the fucking love of my life whether he knew it or not. He studied my face.

"That what you want?" he asked me quietly, knowing exactly where I'd set my mind.

"Yes."

"I'm game," he said, holding my gaze.

A thrill shot through me, giving me a sense of life, I'd fucking missed.

"What can I bring?" Jill asked, her voice unsteady and small.

I tore my focus off Kane's face. "Just your beautiful self—unless you prefer something other than beer."

"Beer's good." Pink still shaded her cheeks as she rubbed her lips together.

"It's a date, then," I said, knowing my eyes glinted.

Neither corrected my choice of words.

KANE

I wanted Charley.

I wanted Jill.

Not knowing if I would ever get to have them the way I wanted, I climbed aboard Charley's idea of a double date of sorts when he made his intentions clear.

Jill wanted Charley, but she wasn't as good at hiding her attraction to him as I was. She stared at his mouth, but unlike me, she didn't know when to look away. She also seemed a little unsure of him, showing that evidence of sheltering herself from him that had lessened with me since the first time I'd met the nervous little bird.

Was it his commanding presence? That aura of power emanating from him? Wait until she experienced fucking him. Women lost their shit over his bossiness, and I counted myself in on that one. He took control, fading everything outside of him from my mind. I'd never experienced being wrecked by him physically, but I'd seen enough to know I wanted it.

Some, like Gracie, preferred my way of things, though—softer, smoother. They lusted for Charley but loved me.

I jerked off in the shower before heading to Charley's, but I still sported a hard-on the whole half-hour it took to get to his Dad's—his place. I wondered if he'd invited us over to take his mind off his grief. If that's how he chose to deal, I sure as fuck wouldn't deny him.

Fuck, I'd do damn near anything to share that intimacy again with him. It'd been over a decade since we'd watched one another while sinking into a woman's body.

Annette had claimed we'd sown our wild oats, but I never felt we'd finished. When it came to Charley, I didn't think I would ever get my fill. If things went the way I hoped, I never would.

Did lungs ever not need oxygen? A body, sustenance?

I would need Charley until I rested six feet under, alongside his twin, the wife I'd lost.

I glanced in my rearview at Jill, who'd insisted on driving herself. To avoid alone time with me? Or to have an escape readily available if Charley made her too uncomfortable?

My protective nature wouldn't allow him to push her, but given the chance, I planned on swaying her our way. I'd never taken advantage of a woman, and I never would, but I had the skills to draw them in.

"You're rusty, you cocky fucker," I muttered to myself as I pulled into Charley's long driveway.

Like my place, his rested deep in the woods, a good ten acres separating him from my childhood home. The distance hadn't stopped me from sneaking over during the night if Charley had gotten into it with his father earlier in the day. A few times, some of my best memories were of us cuddled close in his bed, my arms around him while he allowed his emotions to loosen. I would press my nose against his hair, breathing him in, my stomach fluttering with feelings I hadn't understood at the time.

I'd been able to label them in our teenage years but knew those emotions rooted in my heart went against the natural way of things. *That* knowledge had changed to the opposite truth with adulthood, but I'd been a chickenshit and decided on the easier choice—Alana.

I glanced toward my parents' place, knowing I would have to stop in soon. I hoped to have Jill or Charley with me. Better yet, both, since the storms of life led me toward the edge of not giving a fuck what people thought.

My parents *would* have a fit if I openly declared myself bi, even if it was only Charley's dick, I couldn't get out of my mind. I'd brushed my knuckles against it a time or two, intentionally unintentional. He'd never jerked away, and I distinctly remembered a groan once. I'd reasoned it away as being the ass he was fucking while we held a woman between us.

Too much to fucking think about.

Blowing out a heavy exhale, I hopped out of my truck, adjusted my semi, and waited for Jill to park. She climbed out wearing a damn cute sundress with the ties of a bathing suit around her neck. I'd told her Charley had a hot tub, and we'd probably end up in it.

Her smile wasn't as steady as I'd come to expect. Nervous little bird had returned.

"Nervous?" I asked with a smile as she moved toward me, the warm breeze fluttering long strands of her dark hair across her face.

"A little."

I took her hand and walked her to Charley's farmer's porch. "Nothing to be nervous about. Just gonna have some drinks, lounge in the hot tub, and not be lonely."

"Charley unsettles me."

"Why?"

She hesitated. "Not sure."

"In a good way or a bad way?"

I felt her side-eye. "Are you seriously asking that after seeing me almost every night this week?"

Might as well stick with honesty. "Yep. And I'm not jealous if that's what you're wondering."

We climbed onto Charley's porch, and I pulled up, grabbing her close, so I could look into her eyes. She rested her hands on my chest while I gripped her hips. How many times had I held her like that, kissing her goodnight? Seven? Eight? I'd seen her almost every night since our first "just friends" date, but we hadn't gone beyond kissing. I hadn't even gotten my hands beneath her clothing, not that I'd tried.

"Look," I told her, "I like you. I'm enjoying the hell out of your company." *Can't wait to enjoy your body if you'll share it with me.* "But I don't have a claim on you. If Charley makes you nervous in a good way, get to know him. He's my brother—I'd do anything for him. So, if that means he gets the girl, he gets the girl." The truth stung, but I knew it in my heart. I'd had my chance at love. Charley hadn't.

"I like you, too, Kane."

Shit. Meaning she liked me in the same way I did her, or she liked Charley, too, as in *also*?

"Just keep an open mind, Jill. Go with your heart. Mine's been crushed, so no need to worry over it."

She stood on her toes to brush her lips over mine. Goddamn, the sweetness … the softness. Made my damn dick hard.

The door opened behind us. "Can I get in on the action?" Charley chuckled, waggling his eyebrows.

Jill's face took on its gorgeous pink sheen as she backed away from me.

"Or let me watch." Charley shrugged. "I'm good either way."

I watched Jill intently to see how she would take his suggestions. Red flushed her from tits to forehead.

"Naughty boy." She let out with a breathy laugh. Her eyes took on a glint I'd seen a time or five when faced with the idea of having both me and Charley. Guess his hinting wasn't too much.

My friend lifted an eyebrow my way. "What have you been telling this woman, Kane?"

It was my turn to shrug, giving him a grin he would recognize.

Shaking his head and laughing, Charley stepped back, motioning us inside. "Come on in..." He leaned down to whisper in Jill's ear as she stepped past him into the foyer, "If you dare."

"Should I be scared?"

He chuckled again and shut the door behind me. "Maybe, little lady."

My nose lifted like a damn bloodhound. Fuck, he smelled good—sandalwood, soap, and all Charley—best fucking smell in the whole damn world.

She followed him through the house, and I followed on her ass, my focus on the round globes beneath her dress.

Charley grabbed a couple of beers from the fridge before leading us into the back yard, surrounded by woods. My body hurt from the long-ass week of work, so I was the first to kick off my sneakers and yank my t-shirt off. I climbed into the hot tub, sinking beneath the steam and heat to hide my boner, letting out a groan.

Charley handed me a beer, and I twisted the cap off, taking a long pull of the cold brew.

Jill pulled her sundress up, and my gaze flitted from Charley's roaming eyes to the skin she uncovered and back again. I'd missed the look of lust in his dark gaze and seeing Jill's taut stomach and tits spilling out of her bikini...

I filled my mouth with beer again to keep from groaning for a whole different reason.

Jill kept her head down, pulling her hair up in a messy bun, somehow tucking it away without an elastic. Long legs carried her over and into the tub beside me, but not close enough. Perhaps she didn't want to give the impression of being with me fully, shutting out Charley.

He ripped his shirt off overhead, and both Jill and I stared.

Fuck. The word drug out in my head and my balls ached. I'd never touched him with reverence as I'd always wanted, but my eyes sure as fuck took their time drinking in the familiar sight of his smooth pecs and cut abs. Forget hiding what I wanted. I couldn't fucking breathe, out of fear I would bust a goddamn nut.

"You keep staring like that, and I'm going to think you're the naughty one." Charley watched Jill, but I felt his words were meant for more than her. Had he seen me eye-fucking him? For the first time in my life, I actually didn't care.

He leaned onto the edge of the tub across from me, meeting my stare before turning his gaze back on Jill.

She scanned the back yard and woods beyond rather than give him her attention, the energy zapping off her body like a live wire.

I pulled her toward me, hoping to lessen the uneasiness rolling off her in waves. "Come here."

She tucked against my side, relaxing against me.

"Okay?" I asked in her ear.

"Yeah."

I took another long pull off my bottle, but it didn't cool my damn blood. "He won't bite—unless you want him to," I told her as the two of them held a staring contest, the damn lust in the air enough to choke me.

She laughed lightly, droplets of water flicking up to land on her face from the jet at my back.

"Tell her about Diane," I said.

Charley laughed, straightening and twisting the cap off his beer. "You want me to talk about old conquests?" Charley drank, so I decided to share the story.

"She had a fetish," I said. "Teeth marks on her body. Our senior year in high school, she was always staring at Charley's mouth. Like psycho staring. Fucking drooling. So, one day, in the middle of health class, she blurts out, she wants him to bite her breast."

"What?" Jill laughed, her gaze flitting between us.

"Cut off the teacher and blurted it out like she and Charley were alone in another dimension, ready to get it on."

Charley swallowed a mouth of beer. "Embarrassed the fuck out of me even though the idea made me hard as hell."

"He's had a biting fetish ever since," I finished for him.

"Don't scare her off, dipshit," Charley muttered with a smirk.

I'd seen those teeth in action … wanted to feel them on my own skin. The thought had me tipping my bottle again to calm my aching balls.

"Kane's always been the gentle one," Charley said, holding my gaze. "Everyone fell in love with him. Even my girlfriends."

"You don't sound jealous," Jill said, dragging his focus off me.

"Why would I be? I fell for him long before the girls did. He was my right hand, my brother in every aspect without sharing blood. Almost like my other half, even though I always felt like something was missing."

Shit. My fucking head whipped toward him as my thoughts twisted to hell. *He fell for me… Other half.*

"He's a good man, Jill. The best if you ask me."

"Are you trying to talk me into your friend, Charley?" Jill let out another breathy laugh, studying the label on her beer.

"I'd like to talk you into both of us. Or, rather, *us* into *you* if you need a clearer picture."

Her head snapped up.

He fucking laid it out on the table—and drank while holding her stare, his stoic mask in place.

Red crept up her neck again as her lips parted.

I didn't know who to look at, whose face to read. My ears rang as I drank down the rest of my beer, my dick hard for both, my heart longing for more than it ought to.

JILL

*W*hat did he just say...?

Both of them.

I might have gulped at the look Charley held me pinned with. I definitely gulped. Fire raced over my skin even as goosebumps pebbled me head to toe. Even if he wanted an answer, I couldn't find the words to express what his suggestion did to my body—tingling, throbbing deep inside me. I opened my mouth and snapped it shut again as JD's whispers of my being a whore rose to my mind.

"I'm not interested in a threesome just because I'm kinky, and you're fucking beautiful," Charley said, breaking the tense silence and ripping my thoughts off my ex. "Kane's had a chance to get to know you. I want the same. Something about you … calls to me, cheesy as that sounds. Even though it sometimes seems you want the ground to swallow you whole, you stand firm, strong. There's fire inside you, a spirit waiting to take flight. I want to be there when you do."

Oh, holy hell. My eyes filled with tears. Charley didn't know me at all, but he *saw* me.

127

"You've given him a chance to prove himself trustworthy," Charley continued, his dark eyes piercing my head, my heart, and my soul. "I'd love the same chance."

Tears slid down my cheeks, but I couldn't find a single word in my head to utter.

Kane squeezed my hand as though he understood my plight.

"I'm asking you to be open," Charley said. "To both of us. Let me be your friend, too. If you want more, I'm on board. If not, I'll respect that. We'll have some drinks, enjoy the night, then you can go home, having gained another friend."

Charley tipped his bottle and finished off his beer, and I squirmed under his stare, intense, dark. I wanted his hands on me, his teeth, but I wanted Kane, too.

Dare I give into temptation and become the whore JD had always accused me of? What were the chances I would have the chance to fulfill that fantasy ever again?

"And if I want two lovers?" I finally whispered, my pulse pounding so hard, I barely managed to voice the question.

"Then I'm sure Kane will agree as readily as me. Your choice. No pressure."

I needed a drink—a double. The cold beer in my shaking hand would have to do. I sucked it down.

"Gonna get us a couple more," Charley said, holding his hand out for my empty bottle. Energy raced up my arm as his fingers grazed mine. He winked and walked away, my stare on his ass, flexing beneath his swimming trunks.

Biteable ass... I didn't have a thing for biting, but Charley's backside, same as Kane's, set my drool factory to work.

He disappeared through the back door into the kitchen.

Kane slid me onto his lap, and I let out a squeak, grabbing his shoulders while settling my legs on either side of his hips. He peered at me, his eyes more brown than green beneath the darkening sky. I wanted to ask him if Charley was what he wanted, or if the two ever interacted when sharing women. There was too much comfort between the two at Charley's suggestion of a threesome for me to be their first.

"What are you thinking?" he asked, his gaze dropping to my mouth, his thumbs rubbing circles on my hip bones.

Can't go there... "I-I don't really know what to think."

"Have you ever been with two men before?"

Oh, the luscious heat sweeping over me. "Um ... not physically, no."

He quirked an eyebrow. "Someone has a naughty fantasy."

Doesn't every woman?

"Have you two ever ... you know." My face heated. "Interacted when with a woman?"

"We haven't fucked, no."

"Touched?"

"Not purposefully, no." He didn't sound happy about that fact.

I chewed the inside of my lip, that fantasy evolving as quickly as lightning. If I was going to do this, I wanted it all. But would either give in to their obvious desire? How could I help them cross that barrier that seemed to set like an oak plank between them?

"Come here," Kane murmured.

We met halfway, our mouths hardly tentative, but I could feel the question between us. Did he want it? Did I? Charley had said it was my decision. He'd called me beautiful. Strong.

Tears stung the back of my eyelids again, and I scooted

closer to Kane, needing his arms, needing the comfort he gave, not just the arousal.

He groaned into my mouth, his hands tightening on my hips as I rocked against his hard length. I'd slept in his bed and woke sprawled across his chest, but he'd been a complete gentleman. I hadn't had a good feel of him until that moment —hard, long. I rocked again, rubbing my throbbing clit against him.

His hands speared into my hair, pulling my knot loose as he lifted his hips to meet my gyrating hips.

"The things you do to me," he groaned into my mouth.

I murmured agreement against his lips, and he pulled back, holding my face in his hands. Silence settled, except for the jets bubbling water around us, and I wanted to drown in his eyes that darkened with lust. He held nothing back from me, never had, from what I could tell. I'd never been a good judge of character before, but I trusted Annette and the emotions I saw swimming in Kane's eyes.

He wanted me beyond the physical, and that truth brought the butterflies to life in my stomach.

"Charley is watching," he whispered, glancing over my shoulder.

That look of infatuation and want didn't lessen in his eyes, and I bit my tongue to keep from asking if he loved Charley. If so, why hide his feelings? It was obvious his friend loved him, too.

"Does he look like he wants to get in on the action?" I whispered back Charley's words from when we'd stood on his porch as nerves trembled my body in Kane's arms.

His gaze moved downward. "He's stroking his dick through his trunks, so I'm thinking, yeah."

My pussy spasmed, and I chewed my inner lip.

"What should I tell him?" Kane asked without taking his eyes off his friend.

"What do *you* want?"

Kane turned back, searching my eyes, his own taking on a glint that curled my toes. "I want to collect my prize from our race the other morning."

Oh lordy, I knew what he wanted, all right. "Tell him to join us." My heart pounded as Kane's gaze darkened.

"You're welcome to join us," Kane said, the rasp in his tone tingling my pussy in the best way possible.

I expected hands on my back, lips on my neck, and when nothing happened, I glanced over my shoulder.

Charley sat across from us, submerged in the bubbling water to his thick pecs, his arms spread along the tub's back, three full bottles of beer set aside. His stoic face returned, replacing the easy-going, chuckling one from earlier, and the heat in his gaze burned my face.

Live, Jill. Be strong, take this moment, and enjoy every second.

I slid off Kane's lap, my legs and arms shaking, my heart in my throat.

Charley reached for me, and I gave him my hand. Strong fingers laced through mine, sending a shot of pure need between my legs as he drew me closer. He tucked our clasped hands behind my back, his other cradling my cheek as I settled on his lap.

Stoic, kinky Charley didn't hesitate, taking my mouth with a hunger that dipped my stomach and swelled my chest full to bursting. Forget gentle swipes of the lips and love-making tongue. Charley took, dominated, owned.

The opposite of Kane yet just as deadly.

I'm a goner. Mad for two men.

Hands gathered my hair, and lips planted on my neck.

Kane.

Oh lordy. I whimpered, and Charley pulled me in tight, grinding his hard length against my core. Fireworks lit, and I grasped his shoulder, his clasp on my other hand sliding down to my ass to hold me tight against him.

Kane moved in, his thighs brushing against my hand, his hands snaking between me and Charley to palm my breasts. One roll of my nipples with his fingers and I shattered, crying out against Charley's mouth.

"Yes," he groaned, biting at my lower lip as I panted. "Come for us, Jill."

My pussy clenched, grasping and greedy, pulsing against nothing. I gulped for air, whimpering as I came down.

Kane's lips slid down my shoulder, his cock grinding against the hand Charley held tight to my ass.

Charley leaned his head back, continuing to lift and grind against my sensitive nub as I caught my breath, soaking in the post-release euphoria. "Want to go inside, little lady?"

Did I dream? "Pinch me."

"Huh?"

"Pinch me," I repeated with barely any tone in my voice. "I think I'm dreaming."

He laughed, a rich rumble in his chest, lighting me up from the inside out.

I want to live.

"Yes." I swallowed. "Take me inside."

Kane pulled me into his arms and hopped out of the hot tub as though I didn't weigh more than a two by four. Soaking wet, he strolled across the cobbled patio, straight into the kitchen, and toward the front where stairs led to the second floor, leaving puddled footprints in his wake.

I glanced around his shoulder to find Charley stalking after us, his tented shorts leading the way, his focus on Kane's ass.

He wanted it, alright.

The image of the two men together flashed through my head, sending a rush of arousal to seep from me.

Kane kicked in a door at the top of the steps, and Charley flicked on the lights but dimmed them slightly.

"How do you want us, Jill?" Kane asked me quietly.

I glanced at Charley, who seemed to be the boss. "I-I don't know." But I did.

Kane set me on my feet, and I only hesitated a second before tugging his soaked trunks down, freeing his straining cock. My mouth flooded with drool at the sight of pre-cum oozing from the slit.

"Lie down, Kane. Let her have her way with you until she comes." Charley's tone pebbled my nipples to hard points.

Kane did as told, his legs dangling off the edge of the bed, and I turned toward Charley. He'd already shoved his trunks down and held his cock in his hand, slowly jacking, his gaze slipping over my trembling body. "Want a condom, little lady, or do you want to take him bare?"

"I'm on birth control, and I've only been with one man," I managed to say past the quaking in my stomach.

One of his eyebrows rose. "Only one man?"

"Ex." I cleared my throat. "My ex," I repeated a bit louder, hating to even bring up that bit of my past.

"Kane?" Charley asked, glancing beyond me.

"Haven't been with anyone in five years. Might blow like a goddamn teenager, but I'm clean, Jill."

"Me, too." Charley met my stare and dropped his dick to move in close, his hands reaching to untie my bikini top. It fell to the wooden floor with a wet splash, and he dropped to his knees, his gaze slipping from straining nipples to my bottoms. Hooking his fingers in the sides, he slid them down my wet legs, and leaned in to swipe his tongue through my dripping slit.

"Oh-oh..." I clutched his head, the short hairs tickling my palms as he took another slow lick.

"Fucking delicious." His low, rumbling tone weakened my legs.

He pulled back to help me step out of the bottoms, but instead of diving back in, he stood in one fluid motion, crowding against my front. "Sit on his dick and take what you want, Jill. I want to watch you fuck him."

Oh, holy hell.

Kane groaned behind me, and I tore my focus off Charley to turn. Kane stroked his length. "Come here."

Yes.

I climbed onto his lap, panting and shaking, my knees settling on either side of his thighs, my gaze snagging on his cut abs.

He pulled me down, smearing pre-cum along my belly before taking my mouth in a searing kiss. So much for gentle. The poor man had gone five years without being inside a woman's body. Was it any wonder he sucked the air from my lungs as his fingers grasped my hair?

I slid my soaked pussy lips along his length, and he groaned into my mouth, oozing more arousal from my body.

I'd never been so turned on in my life. Kane's mouth and the thought of Charley watching—wetness dripped from me.

Kane tugged me higher and notched against my opening. Pulling away from my lips, his pupils eating the green of his eyes, he waited, his palms cradling my face. His self-control turned me on as much as the trembling body beneath me—hard as a rock, pure muscle, and smooth skin.

I pressed back, impaling myself, our gazes latched as he buried deep against my womb, his thumbs caressing my cheeks.

"Holy hell," I gasped at the same time he hissed a curse.

Jaw clenched, he pulled out and rammed back into me.

I grasped his shoulders, my mouth falling open at the sweet ache deep inside.

"Move with me," he said, his hands tangling in my hair and tugging me back to his mouth. "Take what you want, just like Charley said."

Our mouths fused again, and I rocked forward and back, dragging my inner walls along his length, and burying him again, all kinds of butterflies and tingles going haywire inside my body. Kane's body inside mine felt right—he filled a part of me I hadn't known sat empty. Emotions rolled over me as our wet bodies slid together, ones I couldn't name, ones that stung my eyelids.

Charley grasped my ass cheeks, holding them wide open.

I stilled, my heart in my throat as Kane owned my lips.

A hot tongue slid over my puckered hole, and I shuddered, moaning into Kane's mouth.

Kane groaned beneath me, his hips taking over fucking since Charley held me still.

"Sorry, but I wanted in on the action," Charley said, not

sounding the least bit contrite, and licked again. "Couldn't fucking wait to taste you."

I whimpered at the lust in his tone and lifted to plank over Kane, my eyes closed and head hanging. He slowly fucked in and out of me while Charley played my ass with his tongue, pressing in and sliding back out, licking and rimming.

"Have you ever had a dick in your ass?" he asked, his finger taking over for his tongue, dipping in and out of me without resistance.

I managed to nod, so damn ready to explode, it wouldn't take much. I hadn't liked having a dick shoved my ass a whole hell of a lot, but wanting two men meant double penetration. That's the way I wanted it—both men, inside my body at the same time.

"Lube?" I asked, my voice shaky as hell.

Charley rounded the bed and pulled a small bottle from his bed stand.

I lifted off Kane's cock, settling onto the bed beside him, my pussy aching the second he slid free. "Will you get him ready for me?" I asked Charley, my voice breathless, my pulse pounding.

He quirked an eyebrow and glanced down at Kane, who tensed between us. "Kane?"

"Give the lady whatever the fuck she wants," he said through grit teeth, his voice shaking and rasped.

Oh, Kane wanted it just as much as I wanted to watch— no doubt whatsoever. If Charley didn't catch that...

The snap of a cap and my gaze glued on Charley's hand and the drizzle he poured on his palm. He grasped Kane's cock without a word, and Kane bowed under his touch, his abs flexing, a gasp ripping from his lips.

Charley jacked him like he'd done to himself.

"Fuck." Kane grasped the comforter and tensed again. "Stop, or I'm gonna blow, Charley. Fuck. Stop. Please."

He likes your hands on him, I wanted to say but kept my lips clamped shut.

Charley stopped and took his own dick in hand, turning to me.

I climbed over Kane's abs, reverse cowboy, taking his slick cock in my hand, working his length, so the back of my thumb rubbed along my slit.

Charley stared at my hand, his own moving in motion with mine. Did he imagine fucking into my pussy or rubbing along Kane's cock?

One way to find out.

"Fuck," Kane muttered beneath me while grasping my hips, and I stilled, holding out my free hand to Charley.

He crowded in close when I wrapped my hand around his dick. A gentle tug brought him flush against Kane and me, his hands fisting at his sides as though the idea of handing control over to me tested his restraint.

I pressed their cocks together, wrapped both of my hands around their combined girth, and jacked them.

"Christ," Charley hissed, his hips moving to fuck against Kane's length.

"Fucking hell, Jill." Kane's tone shivered over my skin, and wetness leaked from my pussy onto his lower abs, flexed tight beneath my ass.

Both men oozed pre-cum, humping into my hands.

I separated them, jacking Charley while rubbing the back of Kane's cock against my pussy. A twist of my wrist placed my palm along the top of Charley's length, and I held his gaze while rubbing the head of his penis all over Kane's drawn-up balls.

Teeth clenched, he watched, his pupils wide, nostrils flared. Tension rolled off him in waves, his shiver leaking more arousal through me.

Kane's legs spread wider, and a thrill shot through me at his silent offering. I pressed Charley's cock head lower, sliding the slickened, flared head over Kane's ass crack.

"Fuck." Charley's hands fisted at his sides, his gaze unwavering from where I rubbed him. "Fucking need to be inside you."

Kane's fingers dug into my hips as he bucked into my hand. "Yes."

I shifted to crouch, positioning Kane's cock against my ass. My breath caught as I pressed down, and I bit my lower lip, forcing myself to relax and let him in. He slid past the ring of muscle, and I winced at the sting.

Charley crowded closer still, climbing over me on hands and knees, like a lion stalking its prey, until I had to straighten my legs and lean back, pressed against Kane's chest, my heels on the bed's edge.

"What's his dick feel like?" Charley asked, his tone haggard while slapping the back of his cock against my clit.

I jolted, and Kane dug his fingers into my flesh, holding me still, his breath hot against my ear as his length twitched inside my ass.

"Thick." I licked at the sudden dryness on my lips. "Hot."

A muscle in Charley's jaw ticked, and he slapped my clit again, jolting me in Kane's hold "Want my dick, too?"

"Yes." I didn't hesitate, overthink, or second guess.

He notched the flared head of his cock inside my pussy, stretching me beyond what I'd thought possible. A slight smirk curled a corner of his lip as he held my stare. "Every inch, Jill?"

I grasped his shoulders and nodded, too overwhelmed by the energy ready to burst into lightning from every cell in my body.

Charley flexed, slowing sinking into me, his thick length shoving against the back of Kane's, fighting for space, a mere membrane of skin apart.

Stuffed. Full.

Holy hell.

"I'm going to come." I gasped as the telltale tingles swept up the back of my legs to settle in my belly. "Going to come—"

Charley thrust and seated deep, ripping the air from my lungs. "Christ, Jill." He peered down between us, dragging his dick back out.

Kane cursed against my ear, his breath hot and shivering my skin with goosebumps.

"Move against me, Kane." Charley pressed back in, and Kane pulled out.

Stars exploded behind my eyes at the combined movement, and a rush of wetness soaked Charley's dick.

"Mmm," he murmured and took my mouth, stifling my cries.

Trapped between two hard bodies, my spirit took flight, soaring high on euphoric waves, shattering into a million pieces, every continued slow drag of their dicks in opposition, prolonging the climax of a lifetime.

I couldn't move. Trapped. Safe in the arms of two men. Riding out my fantasy.

Another climax rose before the first ended, and I writhed, crying out.

Charley planked over us and thrust with purpose, and Kane followed suit, moving faster. Harder.

Holy fucking hell...

I held Charley's shoulders, my fingernails digging in, my eyelids clenched shut. With the first pulse of his dick inside my body, he bit down on my neck hard enough to sting—hard enough to send me soaring again.

Kane grunted, his fingers bruising my hips, and a shudder rippled through me as their dicks spasmed together, filling me with shots of wet heat. My ears rang as I fought for breath, a sweating pile of lax muscle and bone.

Charley's teeth gave way to his lips and soothing tongue, licking at the sweat on my neck and gently biting my chin.

Kane pressed his nose beneath my ear and gave one last sigh, his body shuddering under me.

Fantasy completed.

My body laid in bliss, but I wasn't anywhere near satisfied. I'd been given a taste and knew nothing and no one would ever compare to what the three of us had shared.

Whore.

For the first time, I didn't give two shits what JD thought. Kane and Charley made me feel beautiful. Strong. Wanted as-is. If wanting more of the two of them made me a whore in the eyes of some, so be it.

I'd chosen to *live*.

'd thought I was going to blow like a damn teen, getting my first hand job. Seeing our dicks together, wrapped in Jill's hands... The heat of him damn near burned me. And her move of rubbing my dick all over his ass, teasing his virgin hole?

Fuck me straight to the goddamn pits of hell.

I'd wanted inside his body since I was old enough to know how men fucked. I'd muttered what I wanted, and Kane's whispered yes, giving me permission to take? The possibility of it being true had seized my balls, and I'd climbed on Jill, needing her around me before I blew my load all over the goddamn bed between their spread thighs.

I'd sunk deep into her body, so wet, so soft. Didn't want to be anywhere else in the world at that moment, but she closed her eyes, and my focus slipped to Kane's face beside hers.

I forgot my fucking name. Couldn't feel anything but the silky clench of her pussy around my dick—she'd sucked me in deeper into *her*. Couldn't tell where I ended, she began, and Kane's gaze caught me up just as deeply.

Three connecting in a way our family and friends wouldn't understand, but it had always been what I wanted. I'd been truthful about loving Kane, yet felt like something was missing. When he'd chosen Alana, I'd lost out.

Jill brought us back together, calming the storm inside me for a time, but waking one of a whole different nature—desire and lust like I'd never known. All-consuming need that would haunt me to the grave.

Would she be open to exploring more? Would Kane?

Hope lit inside me, but I had to be the first to detangle myself from the sweating flesh and grasping hands.

Jill whimpered as I slipped free, my cum oozing from her swollen pussy lips. I wanted to shove it back in like a goddamn caveman, but Kane slid her chest up along his back, easing his dick from her ass. My cum joined with his, dripping from both of her holes onto his abs. The musky scent of sex filled my nose, and I breathed it deep into my lungs, the sight of their sprawled forms filling me with a sense of accomplishment—of rightness.

"Shower, anyone?" I asked, holding my spent dick in my hand.

"Can't move," Jill whispered, a soft smile on her lips, her dark lashes feathering her cheeks.

I dropped my dick and gathered her limp body in my arms. Beneath the scent of sex and sweat, the subtle hint of expensive perfume rose from her heated skin. I wanted to drown in the scent, douse it over my goddamn head.

Kane led the way to the bathroom, and I watched his ass flex with each step.

While my shower wasn't exactly large enough for three adults, we made do, me washing Jill's back while Kane took care of her front. A few maneuvers and a lot of laughter accompanied Kane and me scrubbing and rinsing, bodies bumping against one another—on purpose on my end, needing to feel the brush of his body hair and hard muscle against me.

We toweled off, and I grasped Jill's hand, leading her back into my bedroom. Full dark filled my window as I tugged off her towel, pulled back my comforter to the foot of the bed, and patted her ass.

"In you go," I told her. "You're staying the night."

"Oh, really?" she tossed back but obeyed, settling on her back, smack dab in the center—right the fuck where I'd wanted her.

"You, too," I told Kane, motioning with my chin toward the far side.

He didn't argue or sass, just crawled in behind her and pulled her back against his front, his face going straight for her neck.

"Any hint of that perfume left on her skin?" I asked, joining them.

"She smells like you," Kane mumbled, licking her collarbone.

Fuck. My dick took a liking to his reaction to the taste of me on her skin, and Kane's gaze shifted to my swelling length. His eyes darkened, and that energy rippled between us as he lifted his gaze to my face.

"Looks like you have a problem," he rasped in his sexy as fuck voice and licked her neck again.

Jill shivered, and I pulled her away from him, flush against my chest. She blinked at me.

"Gonna let you rest, little lady. I won't let the big bad wolf get you."

"You're the one who bites," she said, her eyes smiling.

"Mmm." I grasped her ass cheeks and squeezed. "True, but I'm not a selfish prick." I kissed her nose and made myself comfortable against the softness of her breasts, one arm banded across her lower back.

Kane moved in, his arm draping across us both. "Okay?" he asked, his gaze on me.

"Yeah."

He laid his head down, and I closed my eyes, soaking in the feeling of his hand on my back, his abs against my fore-arm, holding Jill tight against my front.

Tucked in … perfectly.

I couldn't even be bothered to get up and cut the dimmers off or pull the comforter over our bodies.

IT WAS STILL dark outside my window when I woke. Jill was plastered to my side, her soft breaths hot against my chest and still steady with sleep.

Kane laid on his back beyond her, the top sheet I'd ripped back with the comforter pulled low over his hips, giving me an eyeful of thick muscles and morning wood. Eyes closed, he appeared to sleep as well.

Had he known I'd spoken to him the night before when I'd said I needed to be inside him? My dick swelled at the thought, and I slid from bed, needing the bathroom. Jill stirred but went back to breathing heavily without waking.

I took a piss and returned to find Kane awake, an arm behind his head, the other stroking his dick as he checked out my naked body. I paused in the doorway and let him drink his fill, thankful I hadn't turned off the light the night before. The boner I'd talked down to empty my bladder returned full force. So much for keeping a mask in place.

Kane knew what he did to me. His eyes said as much as his gaze met my face.

Fuck.

My balls ached in a flash, and I found myself stalking to his side of the bed. I'd had enough pussyfooting around and denying the attraction I'd felt for him since we were kids.

I wanted to touch. I was *going* to touch.

Yanking the sheet off his groin, I slid into bed beside him. Our stares locked, both our breaths ragged as fuck.

"Charley..."

I grasped my hand atop his on his dick. "Let me."

He removed his hand, and I wrapped my fingers around his length. A hiss escaped him, and he bit his lower lip, abs contracting as I squeezed like I would my own dick.

Pre-cum oozed from his slit, and I slicked my hand, smearing it down his length. He thrust into my hold and groaned.

Crowding in close, I pressed my front against his side. "Roll," I whispered in his ear, and like a good boy, he did as told, giving me his ass crack to rub against. My own pre-cum smeared him good and slick, giving me the perfect place to rut against while jacking him off.

"I've always wanted this," I growled by his ear, my eyes on Jill's unmoving back.

"Fuck," he groaned, another swell of pre-cum dribbling from his dick.

Jill didn't twitch, not that I'd have cared if she did. The way she'd teased me with Kane's body the night before, she must have read the lust between us.

My balls drew up tight, and Kane grasped his hand atop mine. A shudder rippled through him as his spunk coated our hands, and a deep groan rumbled his chest.

Fuck, yes.

I closed my teeth over the hard muscle in his shoulder and thrust along his ass crack, my own cum erupting between us.

Heaving for breath, we both stilled, our hands clasped together around his dick.

"I've always known I wanted you," I whispered and pressed a kiss against the slight indent of teeth marks I'd left on his skin.

"It's not right," he whispered back.

"It can be."

KANE

Charley and I drank our coffee, standing in his kitchen, our gazes plastered on each other's faces. What the fuck had happened? How had the walls I'd kept so carefully constructed been demolished?

Jill.

She'd brought out a side of us both had hidden for so long. Charley's words still rang in my ears—they had since he'd left me in his bed to clean up. I'd gone into the bathroom after him, Jill still passed out.

I've always wanted this.

How had I not known? Stoic fucker never let anyone inside, but Jill had cracked his facade, figured him out in a matter of hours when I'd had years and failed. And I'd thought I'd known him inside and out. I didn't know what the fuck to say or where our paths led since we'd crossed a barrier I'd never dared to hope for.

The stairs creaked, drawing our attention to the stairwell. Jill came down, her dark hair a waterfall around her face as she watched where she stepped.

"Coffee?" Charley offered, and she glanced up, her attention flitting from one of us to the other. Paleness replaced the usual pink on her cheeks.

"Come here, beautiful," I said, setting my mug aside and holding out my arms.

She hugged herself with one arm while grabbing her purse off the table. "I really gotta go."

Shut down, wanting the floor to swallow her whole—I'd thought I'd gotten past that part of her.

Charley stared long and hard at her, his brow furrowed.

She wasn't sleeping...

I jerked back toward her, guilt slamming into me like a goddamn sledgehammer.

"I-I'll call you later." Jill turned and walked away as we stood and stared after her like a couple of buffoons.

The fuck?

Charley took a step to go after her, but I grabbed his arm. "Let her go."

"What the fuck, man—"

"Confrontation isn't going to do jack shit. Let her go."

His shoulders slumped, and he leaned against the counter.

The front door snicked shut.

"We fucked up," I muttered, scrubbing a hand down over my face.

"The fuck we did," Charley shot back. "This has been a long time coming."

I eyed him, my lips pressed tight. He didn't know Jill like I did and didn't understand her trust issues. If she knew our feelings for one another like I thought she did, she'd be thinking she didn't belong. That we'd done something behind her back, which we literally had done.

"I'll talk to her," I said, heading to the back door to get my shirt and shoes out by the hot tub where we'd left them the night before. "Find out why she's upset. She trusts me."

"You can't walk away from me right now, Kane. Not now, not like this."

I paused in the doorway without turning. "She's running from something, Charley, and I like her. I'm not gonna let her take off again because of whatever shit is poisoning her damn head."

"I want to talk to her, too."

"Later. Trust me in this."

He didn't stop me from leaving. "At least fucking call me after, so I'm not left wondering what the fuck all goddamn day long," he hollered after me.

"Will do."

I drove away from Charley Woodhill's house, the feel of his hands and teeth lingering on my body, my heart torn, my mind a fucking mess.

What option did I have? While Charley had owned part of my heart for years, Jill had weaseled her way in and kickstarted my protective instincts, capturing a piece of me I didn't know I had left to give.

I wasn't about to give her up, but I couldn't stand the thought of putting Charley aside again, especially after what we'd shared that morning.

Truck windows open, I breathed in the cool morning air, the wind ruffling my hair.

Alana didn't speak to me as I strained to hear her thoughts on what I ought to do. She was gone.

It was time to move on—but with whom and how?

JILL'S CAR wasn't parked at the store, so I continued up the road, hoping like fuck she went to her thinking rock. Knowing her head must be as full as mine with conflicting thoughts, I expected that's where she'd gone. Sure enough, her car was parked on the wide berm, and I pulled to a stop behind her as far off the road as I could get.

I found her, knees drawn up, hugging herself atop the rock where we'd sat the Monday before.

She glanced at me and away again as a branch broke beneath my foot.

"Can I join you?"

"Yes." Her whisper reached me over the swishing sounds of the swift-moving water below.

I perched beside her, my legs dangling over the rock, careful to give her space since she hugged herself tight. My stomach was in knots, but I couldn't give her time. I needed to know what thoughts had sent her running—and why. How I could overcome them. Make things right.

"Why'd you take off like that?" I asked, keeping my tone soft instead of barking like Charley would have done, demanding answers.

Lips pursed, she stared over the stream, a slight frown denting her brow. "Tell me about Charley, Kane," she said, ignoring my question.

I knew what she wanted and found I didn't want to hold back what I'd secreted away, my entire damn life. Maybe my being vulnerable would give her the strength to do the same.

"I've loved him since I met him," I said and swallowed against the sudden ache in my throat. "But that sort of love isn't acceptable around these parts. I pushed it down deep inside, making myself content being his friend. Sharing women when we were younger, afforded me the intimacy I craved, but eventually, I knew I would need to choose someone else. Alana was so much like him..." My throat closed off, the view of the trees across the water hazing as tears filled my eyes as I fiddled with Nat's bracelet around my wrist.

Jill lowered her legs beside mine and grasped my hand.

We sat in silence for a few minutes while I got ahold of my damn emotions.

"She wasn't second best," I whispered.

"You loved her, too."

"Yes." I blew out a heavy exhale and squeezed her fingers. "I'll want him until the day I'm six feet under, but I'm a greedy bastard, Jill. I like women, too. Especially you."

She sat silently, not giving me her thoughts, even though I craved them as much as I did her lips.

"Jill?"

She finally turned to face me, her big brown eyes full of sadness.

I cupped her cheek, studying her eyes, trying to figure her the fuck out. "Did I fuck everything up with you?"

Her slight hesitation said more than enough. "No. I-I just felt like I was intruding on something I figured had been a long time coming."

"You weren't intruding, Jill. We both wanted you there."

She didn't respond.

"How did you know? About him and me when no one else around here has figured it out?" I asked quietly.

"The way you two look at one another." She shrugged and turned her attention back on the stream again. "It's obvious as water is wet."

I wanted to say I was sorry—but I wasn't. *Fuck*. I scrubbed a hand down over my face. "Can I make you breakfast?"

"I think I'm going to sit here for a while if that's okay," she whispered, not meeting my gaze.

"Of course, it's okay. Just don't go running off with that piece of my heart you've stolen."

Jill dropped her head, her hair shadowing her face from view. "I won't. Promise." A smile laced her whisper.

While I hadn't gotten the answers I wanted, I took comfort in trusting she wouldn't light out for places unknown.

"Call me later?" I felt like a needy, whiny ass for asking but couldn't leave without that assurance.

"I will."

I left Jill sitting on her rock, my stomach still as hard as one. Rather than call Charley as I'd promised, I shot him a text after climbing into my truck, letting him know she wasn't going anywhere, but we'd have to be patient until she wrapped her head around what had happened between the three of us. I just hoped like fuck she didn't take too long to give me—or Charley—another shot. She'd gotten under my skin, weaseled into my heart somehow, and the thought of losing her didn't sit well. At all.

JILL

I'd feigned sleep, listening to Charley jerk off Kane, my body hot as hell, wetness swelling between my thighs. I'd held still, listening, imagining—biting my lip to keep from moaning—allowing them their first moment alone together.

Kane's whispered words of their not being right and Charley's response of it being possible had meant one thing to my mind—non-inclusion of one new-to-town girl named Jill. The thought stung, and I'd swallowed against tears as the men slipped from the bed to clean up. When neither returned, their footfalls and the creaking stairs, letting me know they crept downstairs, the thought solidified.

They'd snuck off, leaving me behind.

I didn't doubt they both had feelings for me, lust at least on Charley's part, even though he claimed he wanted to get to know me, but the two men had history. A shit ton of it from what I'd gathered. Finally, having that wall broken down between them, one of my own doing, I expected they would want to explore fully and find what their hearts had wanted all along.

I sat on the rock for over an hour, my lack-of-caffeine headache dragging me back to civilization.

I'd partially been at fault, rubbing the two men together, taking them past the point of hiding what they'd both wanted for so long. But hadn't I wanted them both to be happy? Wasn't that my intention from the moment I saw the longing between them? I achieved that, so why did my chest ache?

I managed to slip up to my apartment unnoticed, and after slugging down my first cup of coffee, I grabbed my cell. I hadn't given Kane any answers, but I wasn't sure what he really wanted.

Me: **Have you talked to Charley?**

Kane's reply came through immediately as if he'd been sitting and waiting for me to reach out. **Texted to let him know you seemed to be okay, but that's it.**

Me: **You two need to talk, Kane. Tell him what you told me. It's obvious as rain, the two of you belong together.**

Kane: **What happened between him and me shouldn't have.**

I frowned. How could he think that? Because of their backward, almost non-existent society in the sticks of bum-fuck Pennsylvania? Because he'd been married to Charley's sister?

Who the fuck cared? If they loved each other, nothing should stand in their way. That kind of longing, Charley's faithfulness to Kane all those years when he was hot enough to have snagged a wife of his own, shouldn't be pushed aside as if it didn't matter—that it *couldn't* matter.

Not sure how to respond, I left it alone for the time being and changed into my jogging outfit. Maybe slapping my feet on the road would settle my mind.

Before the first mile passed beneath me, I realized what I needed to do. Since something held Kane back from figuring things out with Charley, I decided I would be the bridge.

ME: **Did you talk to Charley?**

I chewed on the inside of my lip while waiting for Kane's reply. It'd been over twenty-four hours since he'd left me sitting on my rock, and I hadn't heard from either of them.

Kane: **Waiting for you to decide what you want.**

Shit.

Me: **I want you happy. I want him happy.**

Kane: **And if that means having you between us?**

Lordy... I didn't know how to respond, but I knew he and Charley needed to figure their relationship out before dragging me into the mix.

I felt like shit not responding, but what could I say that wouldn't sound like manipulation? Seeing proof in text, they needed a bridge, I made my way to Charley's house that night after a full day of Annette watching me like a hawk. She didn't ask, surprisingly, and I didn't tell.

Kane hadn't texted to press for an answer. Giving me space, or letting me go?

I hated the idea of both, but I wanted to be a bridge, not a wedge or a stumbling block to keep the two men apart.

I pulled up to Charley's big house, my heart in my throat as I parked alongside his truck. The sinking sun still lit the meadow, shots of pink and purple streaking the sky overhead.

He opened the door and waited for me on the porch, his face a mask. I'd hoped for the joking, smiling Charley, but no such luck.

My legs trembled as I approached, my smile faltering. "Can we talk?"

"Of course." He motioned me inside, and I stepped past him, filling my lungs with the scent of sandalwood. Arousal rose, but I mentally shoved against it, wiping damp palms down my jean shorts.

"Drink?"

"Sure," I croaked out.

"Have a seat. Be right back."

I stared after his ass in the gray sweats hanging on his hips. Those pants ought to be illegal. The second he disappeared into the kitchen, I moved into the living room and perched on the couch's edge.

He returned with two bottles of beer, stealing the oxygen from the room as his dark eyes plastered to mine. Without a word, he handed one over and sat beside me, lounged back, one arm propped along the back of the couch, his fingers inches from my hunched shoulders.

"Thanks," I whispered and wet my whistle.

"So, what's going on in that pretty little head of yours, beautiful?"

I couldn't help my smile, my insides growing warm. "You and Kane."

"More fantasies?" His eyes joked though he didn't smile.

"Shut up."

Charley's face relaxed, and he chuckled, taking a sip of his beer. "Spill, little lady."

"How are you doing?" I asked, studying his face. For having just lost his father, he didn't seem to be in grieving. He certainly hadn't, the night we'd shared a bed.

"I'll be better once you tell me why you lit out of here yesterday morning."

He didn't want to talk about his father's passing, no problem, but I couldn't be the one to declare Kane's love for him. That he needed to hear straight from Kane's delicious mouth. I could only plant the seeds to set their love in motion.

"I heard what you told Kane yesterday morning, and I agree you're right for each other," I told him, studying his face. "Looking at the two of you, it's like you're two parts of a whole. I don't want to get in the way of what you've both been fighting for years."

His face remained relaxed, but his eyes took on a glint that tightened my stomach, damn him. "I've always wanted to be two parts—of three," he murmured. "But Kane chose Alana. And now I might have a chance with him, but I want you both."

I gulped and fought off the shiver wanting to lick down my spine. "You don't know me."

"I think I made it pretty damn clear I want to."

"You would risk finally having the opportunity to explore things with Kane over a woman you've only just met?"

"Kane wants you just as much as I do, Jill." His gaze dropped to my lips. "Trust me on that."

I chewed the inside of my lip, somehow able to keep from looking away from him as his gaze lifted to my eyes again.

"Hungry?" he asked, and I blinked, wondering at his

meaning. He chuckled, relieving the sudden tension that had tightened my shoulders. "I was just about to grill some chicken. Want to make the salad?"

"S-sure," I managed, standing when he did.

Charley slid his fingers through mine and tugged me toward the kitchen. "So, it's a date-date, none of this 'just friends' shit you and Kane play at?"

My mind went straight to his best friend. "Think he'll mind?"

"Nope, but you can text him and ask if it'll set your mind at ease."

I did just that as Charley pulled a pack of chicken breasts from his fridge, my fingers shaking while flying over the screen.

Me: **Would you mind if I have dinner with Charley?**

My cell dinged within seconds.

Kane: **Not at all, but I'm a little jealous.**

Me: **Over who?**

Kane: **Both of you. Enjoy yourselves.**

Me: **Can I call you later?**

Kane: **If Charley lets you out of his bed before midnight.**

Oh, lordy. Trembles broke out through my body. *This is so ... weird.* Two men, zero jealousy, one very horny, whorish woman—trouble or paradise? Tension strung me tight at the thought I wasn't building a bridge at all—but both men seemed to want exactly what my body did.

"You okay?"

Charley's question jerked my head up. He studied me, concern in his eyes.

"Y-yeah." I forced a smile, my pussy spasming at the thought of being beneath him again.

"What'd Kane have to say?"

My face heated fully. "To enjoy ourselves."

Charley's slow smile licked shivers down my spine and throbbed through my clit. "We'd best do as he says, then, yeah?"

I nodded like an idiot, unable to find my voice.

"Salad stuff is in the fridge," he said, turning toward the back door for the grill beside the hot tub. "Make yourself at home, little lady."

Once he disappeared from sight, I managed to move my legs.

He returned when I had his veggie drawer emptied onto the counter as I hunted for a cutting board and knife.

"Here." He pulled open a lower cabinet and handed me the board. "Knives are in the drawer to your left."

I set to work, and he placed two bowls beside me.

"Your hands are shaking," he murmured, brushing against me.

"You make me nervous," I whispered, keeping my focus on the cucumber I sliced.

"Hopefully, in a good way."

I smiled, remembering my conversation with Kane over that very thing. "Yeah," I murmured, admitting to the tingles racing through me.

"Good," he whispered against my ear. "Because you make me nervous in a good way, too."

I snorted.

"Don't believe me?"

"Nope."

He grabbed the hand holding the cucumber, and placed my two fingers against his neck. His pulse throbbed beneath his warm skin. I stared into his dark eyes as he allowed me to *see* him as he *saw* me. A slow smile lifted my lips, and his gaze dropped to them.

Unlike Kane, Charley didn't ask—he took with one quick swoop of his head, stealing my breath with a hungry kiss. The knife clattered to the counter, and he hiked me up, setting my ass next to the cutting board, shoving the other veggies out of the way.

He ate my mouth like a man starving for life, for breath, stealing mine, and swallowing my whimpers. Grasping my ass, he pulled me close, so my breasts smashed against his hard chest. He had no hair to grasp, so I went for the muscles of his shoulders, hanging on for dear life.

"You're so goddamn delicious, Jill," he groaned into my mouth and swept his tongue along mine again as though searching for more of my taste. "Like a sweet strawberry with just enough tart to make me crave more." Heaving for breath, he tipped his forehead against mine, his palms hot against my cheeks.

"Dinner," he croaked out as though reminding himself he'd invited me on a date, not a fuck fest. I opened my mouth to argue, but his words kept me silent. "Not going to rush this and fuck it up. Let's do it right, okay?"

He pulled back to study my face again, a determined glint in his eyes. "We're going to sit and talk, get to know each other like we should have done before I talked you into a threesome the other night."

"I didn't mind," I offered him the truth in my heart.

A crooked smirk tilted his lips. "Nice to know, but let's

start over. After I get the chicken on the grill." He tugged me off the counter. "I like extra carrots," he said before striding away. "And my tomatoes cut small."

I smiled after him—bossy bastard. Turning back to the counter, I set to work, making him a salad to die for.

A half-hour later, he pulled out my chair for me at his dining room table.

"So, tell me all about you," he said, serving me one of the steaming breasts he'd brought in.

Shit. I should have known he'd get nosey. The whole get to know each other, never mind he worked in law enforcement. "What do you want to know?"

"Where you're from. What brought you up here? Why you're so goddamn beautiful and still unmarried."

"I could say the same about you, you know," I shot back, avoiding the topic of me as usual.

A twinkle lit in his eye. "You think I'm beautiful?"

"More like hot as hell," I admitted, heat rising to my cheeks. I reserved the word beautiful for Kane.

Charley all-out grinned, flipping my belly in the best way possible. "You're avoiding the questions."

"And you're nosey."

"I like your sass, Jill." He reached under the table as though adjusting himself, and even more heat rushed to my face.

"How much?" I pushed, keeping our conversation in semi-safe territory since I enjoyed the butterflies in my belly.

"A lot." His dark gaze said it all. I would end up in his bed, just as Kane suggested. "So, now you're going to answer my questions and let me get to know you better."

I took my time cutting a piece of chicken and shoving it into my mouth, my stare on my plate.

"Troubled past?" Charley wasn't going to let it go.

"A little," I whispered once I swallowed, reaching for my glass of water to help the sudden dryness in my throat.

"Anything I need to know?"

"No."

Silence rose long enough, I dared a glance upward to find him studying me again. I shifted on the chair.

"I won't pry, Jill," he said, "but if you ever need anything, you let me know, okay?"

Tears clogged my throat, and I nodded.

His soft smile eased the tension that had replaced the butterflies in my stomach. "If it doesn't matter to us what brought you here, then I won't push. You want to share, you share. If not, I won't be hurt or offended. It's your past to know, not mine."

"Thank you," I managed to whisper.

Charley turned his attention on his salad bowl and pulled it closer, eyeing my masterpiece. "Damn, woman. You're good."

I eased back in my chair, a hint of a smile lifting my lips. Praise—simple edification over a mere salad—never sounded so sweet.

A few hours later, darkness smothered the sky beyond Charley's kitchen windows. We'd sat in the hard chairs, talking non-stop, having a few too many beers. While I didn't know Charley as well as Kane, I certainly had a brain full of stories. We shared a lot of laughter while washing up the dishes, more than a fair share of heated stares after we sat again. I even admitted to having grown up in western Maryland and that both my parents had passed within six months of one another, same as I'd done with Kane.

We spoke of grief, of the storms of life that had stolen from our hearts. My biggest storm, my biggest regret, however, I kept to myself—no sense in bringing up the shit that had torn me down and taken advantage of my grief over losing my parents.

Charley sat back in his chair, hands on his thighs, his empty beer bottle on the table in front of him. "Want to take things to the living room?"

I glanced at the clock on his wall—ten. I had to work the next morning and didn't want to miss my jog as the sun rose. "I ought to get going."

"Stay the night with me, Jill."

My teeth found the inside of my lip as I considered his words.

"Kane said to enjoy ourselves, and I'm all aboard that train," he continued in his low, rumbling voice. "I want you in my bed, in my arms, beneath me, on top of me. I just want *you.*"

So, not the cuddling Kane had insisted on the night he'd made me dinner.

"Stay the night with me," Charley repeated, bossy and stoic, although his eyes betrayed his awareness of the sexual energy between us.

Whore.

I gulped, pushing JD's whisper from my head. Reminding myself I wanted to live, I nodded. "Okay."

CHARLEY

I took my time stripping Jill down. She stared up at me with huge eyes, lips parted, and pulse thrumming in her neck, the same as mine. Anyone would think we would feel guilty, but Kane had given his blessing. I knew he wanted what I did, but did he want it long term?

Being with him and Jill together had been perfection, and I wanted more—a hell of a lot more. I had a taste of the perfect man/woman combo in my bed, and I had every intention of it happening again and again.

But first, I had to learn Jill's body and explore the connection zapping between us without Kane's influence.

The weight of her breasts fit my hands, her nipples tight buds between my fingertips. She gasped when I pinched, her hands grasping my forearms, but her brow didn't furrow, so I squeezed again, causing a shudder to ripple through her.

"Lie down for me, little lady," I whispered against her ear. "Let me make you feel good."

Jill climbed onto my bed, her breasts jiggling as she scooted to the center.

I pulled off my shirt and shoved my sweats down, my hard-on springing free and slapping upward against my abs. Her gulp twitched my lips and bounced my dick again, but I prowled up and between her legs, my focus on heaven—dark hair, neatly trimmed and swollen, pink lips, separating as I pressed her thighs wide, the glistening hole between rushing drool to my mouth.

"Fucking beautiful," I groaned and sank my teeth into the inside of her thigh.

Jill gasped but didn't pull away.

I bit her other thigh, and she groaned, her pussy spasming.

The little lady liked my teeth—*fuck, yeah.*

I flicked my tongue, gliding through the creamy wetness, seeping from her pussy. Tangy and sweet, her arousal coated my tongue, and I wondered how Kane would taste. Wetness leaked from my dick onto the bed as I settled into feast, Jill's moans and her grasp on the sides of my head spurring me on.

Every flick of my tongue over her clit jerked her in my hold, every slow lick from asshole to contracting pussy had me wanting to bury balls deep. I lifted my gaze to her tipped back head and parted lips, teasing her entrance with the tip of my middle finger.

"Please, Charley."

"What do you need?" I pushed into the first knuckle and retreated, sliding up to circle her nub.

"I want you inside me," she whimpered, shifting her hips. "Please."

I gave her my middle finger, rubbing along the inside of her hot, slick wall. "Like this?"

"More."

I sucked my other middle finger, lubing it up good for her ass, and slowly pressed in, dragging my other from her pussy.

"Yes..." she whispered and moaned as I worked both holes, her arousal dripping off my knuckle to coat my finger shoving into her tight ass.

"So wet." I watched myself finger fuck her, my balls drawing up tight. "Slick and hot. Fuck." I latched onto her clit, sucking and flicking.

"Charley—"

I found her g-spot, biting down on her clit hard enough to sting, and she bowed off the bed, shrieking and squirting all over my chin and hands.

"Oh God... oh God..." She thrashed and gulped, her pussy squeezing the hell out of my finger, her ass tight around the other.

The second she calmed, I pulled back, wiped my face on the sheet beside me, and returned to her torso, kissing, licking, and biting my way up to her breasts. A few love bites, hard enough to leave indents in her soft skin, brought more whimpers to her lips. She grasped my head and yanked me upward, and I gave her my mouth, rubbing the back of my dick up over her pussy.

"Need you," she whispered against my lips.

I gave her all nine inches with one slow thrust, erupting groans from both our chests as I rested against her womb. Time warped—stood still as we shared breaths, my heart pounding in my ears.

Mine.

The thought solidified in my heart as I drowned in her

dark pupils, the subtle scent of spice and Jill sucking me in deep, latching my soul onto hers.

"Yes." She held my face as I tipped my forehead to hers, our eyes glued to each other as I fucked in and out, every drag and thrust of my dick through her soaked heat, tingling my balls, binding me tighter to her.

"Gonna fucking blow like a goddamn teenager, Jill. Fuck." I peered down between us, watching my creamed-up dick disappear inside her body. "You feel so fucking good." Lowering, I took her mouth again, my hips moving on their own, my body taking over in its need for release.

Jill writhed beneath me, lifting her hips to meet my every thrust, her soft mewling against my mouth the biggest fucking turn on ever. Reaching between us without losing rhythm, I found her little nub and thrummed the hell out of it with my thumb.

"Come around my dick, Jill. Suck me in deep—give it all to me."

Your mind, your heart—your soul.

Her eyelids flicked upward, and I drowned in the need filling her gaze as she clenched down on my dick.

"Charley," she croaked my name and came.

I held her gaze as the first burst of cum shot from my dick, deep inside her. A deep groan tightened my throat, and I pumped again, giving her another spurt ... and another, and a fucking fourth, her sweet pussy milking me dry, sucking everything I had to give, deep inside her.

I'd fucked plenty of women, but I'd never stared into their eyes while emptying my balls inside their bodies. Like two wisps of smoke coming together, dancing, mingling to the point they become one entity, our spirits seemed to become one.

My heart pounded, my abs clenched tight.

Buried deep and still hard, I fought for breath, fucking lost in her warm gaze.

A soft smile tilted her mouth upward, and she rubbed her thumb over my lower lip.

Fuck, this woman...

I gave her my mouth, crushing our chests together, my arms twining beneath her body. A swift roll settled her atop me, sending a cascade of dark hair around our heads.

I had no fucking words, had no wish to be anywhere else at that moment but connected to Jill, physically and emotionally. The only one to make my dick hard to the point of pain until that day had been Kane.

I gyrated my hips beneath her, the sticky mess of our cum leaking down over my balls, without a doubt, making a mess on my bed, but I couldn't find it within me to give a fuck. If Kane had been with us, I'd have told him to lick me clean. I wondered if he would, the thought seizing my balls up tight again.

Jill squeezed her inner muscles around my semi, and I clenched my teeth, groaning.

"Feel good?"

"Fuck, yes." I grasped her hips and shifted her forward and back over my hardening dick, quickening the slow, lazy rhythm she'd taken up.

"So do you."

She smiled down at me, her breasts swaying, nipples scraping against my chest.

"Come again for me," I told her, rubbing her clit all over my lower abs and pelvis.

"Are you always this bossy?" she murmured, still smiling and riding my dick like a goddamn pro.

"Always."

"I'm not going to come again any time soon," she told me, serious as fuck.

I rolled her beneath me again—and fucking proved her wrong within two minutes. She gave me another, seconds later, and I finally gave into my balls' need to fill her up again.

MY SHAFT ACHED inside my sweats. My lips and tongue pretty much the same. We'd spent three hours in my bed, sucking, licking, and fucking until exhausted. Jill refused to stay the night, claiming she needed her early morning jog before work. I didn't want her driving that late, but she said she'd been doing so since her parents allowed her out overnight.

Parents I hadn't learned about other than they'd passed within six months of one another. She'd stayed close-lipped over her past, but I hadn't pushed. With how much I enjoyed being with her, I knew it wouldn't be anywhere near the last time. She would come to trust me and eventually, tell me the secrets of her past.

I ended up on my porch, propped against one of the porch pillars beneath a black sky, watching her taillights disappear down my driveway, an ache rippling over my chest.

Never having known such release, such complete fucking satiated bliss, I crawled into my bed on one side, avoiding the mess we'd made on the other, too damn tired to change the sheets.

My eyes closed, but I clutched my cell atop my bare chest, waiting for Jill's text. I refused sleep, thinking I should have forced her to stay with me rather than drive, and twenty minutes later, she let me know she'd locked herself up tight in her apartment.

I wished her goodnight, thanked her for one of the best of my life, and rolled over, giving up to exhaustion and relief, she'd made it home safe and sound.

I FLICKED on the news like I did every morning while waiting for the coffee pot to finish brewing. A woman's image popped onto the screen, one with a fuller face and heavier makeup than I'd had in my bed the night before, but I knew those eyes. Dreamed about their dark depths.

Jill Walters. Missing since the previous fall. Another image—a full-figured little lady, one I doubted too many of the locals would recognize.

A fifteen-hundred-dollar reward for any tip that led to her being found...

"Fuck." I scowled and watched as her husband cried, begging for help to find his wife—the love of his life, his other half he couldn't live without.

I flew out the door half-dressed, without coffee, my stomach a rock, my scowl etched in stone.

Fucking married.

And, if my instincts could be trusted, to an abusive asshole, who played to the goddamn cameras. Jill had curled in on herself one too many times. Shied away if I'd leaned too close those first two times we'd met. She wouldn't even meet my gaze head-on and hold it until we'd fucked.

Even so, I felt lied to and couldn't fucking stand that fact.

I caught sight of her tight ass in running shorts heading south, same as me. She moved off the road as I approached, but I slowed—and she sped up. Lowering the window, I called out to her, and she jerked her head toward me, the fear in her eyes dissipating the second she saw it was me, crawling up her ass like a creepy stalker in a big fucking truck. I stopped, and she did too.

Knowing I had to keep my tone in check, I tried not to bark when I said, "Get in."

Brow furrowing, she did as told, sucking wind, her face pink and sweaty. Fuck, she looked good.

"JD is looking for you."

Sheet white replaced the color in her cheeks. "Wh-what?"

"Your husband."

Jill blinked and swallowed. "Ex," she whispered, her shoulders wilting as though the weight of the world settled on her.

"He seemed pretty adamant you were still together."

"Because he refuses to accept the fact the judge granted me a divorce last year," she whispered, still fighting for breath—with a hint of bite to her tone rather than curling in on herself, thank fuck.

I studied her face, and she lifted her chin, showing me the backbone she must have grown since leaving his ass.

"He hurt you."

She nodded and swallowed. "Yes."

"How bad?"

"Only with words until I was granted the divorce, and he found me hiding out at my friend's house. Then he put me in the hospital, but I lied about the bruises because he hovered. Watched me like a damn hawk."

I clenched the steering wheel as the need to throttle the fucker swept through me. "How did you escape?"

"His father needed him back at the family business."

A car approached in the rearview, so I let off the break and started down the road again.

"How long were you in the hospital?"

"Five days."

"Fuck." He'd beat the shit out of her to stay that long. I couldn't fucking focus on that fact, or I'd lose my shit.

"The minute he left," Jill continued, her voice small, her breathing evened out, "I told my nurse the truth. She pushed me to press charges, but I begged for her to turn away. Let me leave."

"Did she?"

"Yes. She also helped me sneak out—among many other things I'll never be able to properly thank her for."

"Where have you been all this time?"

"Running. Hiding. Trying to learn to live again—without fear."

"Obviously, he wants you back. Think he'll come looking?"

"I-I don't know," Jill whispered, hugging herself again and turning her gaze out the passenger window. "But his family has money. You've heard of Walter's Fine Furniture?"

"His family's?"

"Yes."

Loaded, for sure. Nation-wide, custom made shit, all the fancy folk needed to outfit their Beverly Hill's mansions.

Shit. The need to wrap her up in my arms and protect her from her shithead ex-husband damn near stole my breath. "Does Kane know any of this?"

"No."

I pulled into the Mountain View Store and swung around the side, pulling up to her little blue car out back. Putting my truck in park, I turned to face her. "He's offering a fifteen-hundred-dollar reward for news of your whereabouts."

She snorted a huffed exhale. "That's it?"

"It's more than enough to get folks around here talking."

Her face paled again, and she hugged herself tighter.

"I almost didn't recognize you in the pictures they showed."

"I was fifty pounds heavier, wore makeup, and frosted my short hair because it's what he liked."

"Still beautiful," I murmured, filling her eyes with tears. "You're one hell of a woman, taking back your life like you did, and I promise I'll have your back. Kane will do the same. Bet my life on it."

"Thank you." A sad smile tilted her lips as a tear slid down her cheek.

"Don't run anymore, Jill. Stay here. I've only just found you—I'm not ready to let you go."

She chewed on the inside of her lip, and I grasped her chin, pulling her toward me while using my thumb to pull her lip from between her teeth.

"Let me do the nibbling, okay? You focus on staying

sharp. Keep those eyes open and take advantage of two men wanting to be with you twenty-four-seven."

"You can't speak for Kane," she said with light laughter, her eyes shining with wetness and a bit more.

"Sure as fuck can. I know that man inside and out."

She studied me, her smile fading. "You thought you did."

I nodded. "You're right, but he didn't shield his emotions when looking at you like he's always done with me. He likes you … a lot. Wants you just as much as I do."

"You do?"

"Thought I made that clear when I begged for you to stay in my bed last night."

Her lips twitched. "Yeah, you kinda did."

"So, are you going to tell Kane?"

"That we fucked or about JD?"

We'd done a hell of a lot more than just fuck, but maybe she wasn't ready to acknowledge that since we'd just met.

"Both," I told her.

"I will."

I squeezed her chin and leaned in to give her a quick brush of my lips. The scent of sweat and me lingered on her skin—fucking divine—and my dick swelled.

"Better get out of here before I beg you to invite me up there," I mumbled against her soft-as-fuck lips.

She let out a throaty giggle, fuck my life, and tore away, hopping from the truck. "I'll tell him," she swore before slamming the door shut. "Promise," she mouthed at me, and I watched her scamper up the stairs to safety.

I scrubbed a hand down my face, my palm scratching over my scruff. Glancing at the dash board's clock, I realized I didn't have time to shower and shave before work. Guess

I'd have to deal with the scent of Jill and her pussy all over my body for my eight-hour shift.

Couldn't find two fucks to give.

At least Annette had a to-go cup of coffee hot and ready for me. Must have seen me pull in. She gave me the side-eye and dropped a few questions, namely why I wasn't wearing a shirt, but I brushed her off.

"Keep an eye on our girl, will you, Annette?"

"She needs looking after?" Annette fished, but I knew she cared enough about Jill, she wouldn't go cashing in on the reward JD had offered.

I nodded, my face hard, and she pursed her wrinkly lips and nodded. "Any man, but you and Kane try to touch her, and I'll put a bullet in him."

Feisty—and accepting. My lips twitched, and I hurried back into the cool morning air.

I had some digging to do on one JD Walters and his ex-wife. I might not carry a cop's badge, but I had the legal right to act like one. If he came looking for Jill, he would end up regretting it for life.

If Annette happened to catch the fucker and did as promised, I'd find a way to make sure it looked like self-defense.

KANE

I swung by the store for coffee. Not that I needed it or had time, but curiosity over what happened between Charley and Jill had kept me up all damn night. Had they fucked? Did she stay the night in his bed, wrapped in his arms, breathing in his warm exhales?

The thought made me hard as fuck, not jealous, even though I wished I'd been there with them.

Her car sat at the base of the stairs leading to her apartment, and the second I pulled to a stop, she pulled the door open, catching my eye. Her face flushed as heat rushed through me, but she didn't smile.

I hopped out, my brow furrowing, and met her at the base of the stairs. "What's wrong?"

She glanced around and motioned back up the stairs with her head. "Can we talk?"

Shit. "I only have fifteen minutes to make it twenty down the road for work, or my bitch boss will can my ass. You okay? I can stop on my way home."

Her smile trembled. "Okay."

"Did that fucker hurt you? I'll rip off his nuts if he did."

"No." She actually let out a small laugh, but the troubled look in her eyes remained. "Charley and I are fine."

"How fine?"

That lush red flooded her cheeks again. "After work."

"I'll make you dinner. Come up to the cabin at six-thirty."

"Okay."

"Bring the bunny food. I'll grab some steaks."

"Sounds good." More laughter escaped her, easing my anxiety over whatever the fuck bothered her.

"Six-thirty," I reminded her, pulling my truck door open again. "Sure you're okay?"

"Yeah. I'll be there!" she called back, and I took off.

I was four minutes late, clocking in. My bitch boss chewed me a new one, and temptation to tell her to go fuck a wooden dowel lay on the tip of my tongue, but I needed the paycheck.

"Make furniture like Jill said, you dumb fuck," I muttered to myself, stalking toward the sawmill. "Learn shit about technology, set up a goddamn website, and figure out how to market what you love doing."

A few hours of similar pep-talk got me stoked to take control of making my own cash, getting out on my own, and earning a living beyond the normal seven-thirty to three-thirty.

Charley texted me two minutes after I sat down to lunch, telling me to call him. I took my bagged lunch outside and sat against a pine.

"You talk to Jill yet?" he asked instead of saying hello when he picked up.

"No." My stomach twisted at the hard tone carrying over the line. "What's up?"

"That past she doesn't want to talk about. I planned to let her tell you, but I've been digging. She's got an abusive ex-husband who's looking for her."

A scowl dented my brow. "Talk."

He filled me in, and I tossed aside my ham sandwich, my appetite gone.

"Five fucking days, Kane," Charley all but hissed. "That means he damn near beat her to death. Paperwork said she'd been mugged and didn't have a clear recognition of the two men who supposedly bashed in her goddamn face."

"Fucking hell," I swore, my heart breaking for Jill, even as rage and the need to punch the shit out of JD Walters, rich boy bastard, fisted my hand atop my thigh.

Just when I thought things might be going my way, that kind of fucking shit had to rise to the surface and put a goddamn damper on my mood.

Selfish prick. Focus on Jill.

I heaved a heavy exhale. "Sure no one will have recognized her from that news bite?"

"Not possible. She had plastic surgery to repair her nose and a fractured cheekbone."

"Fuck."

"Lost a shit ton of weight and grew out her natural hair. If not for those whiskey eyes, I wouldn't have recognized her, either."

Fine as fuck eyes...

"Call me if you hear anything, yeah?" I told him, my scowl firmly in place.

"Promise. And, Kane?"

"Yeah?"

"We need to talk, too. About all the shit we've been hiding from one another."

"Yeah," I agreed quietly, watching as the other workers filed out of the lunchroom's back door. "I'll give you a call. Gotta go, lunch is over."

I hung up, feeling as shitty as when my bitch boss had reamed me a new one.

I had dinner with Jill to look forward to. I expected what I'd learned was what she wanted to talk to me about. At least Charley had warned me, so I wouldn't go punching a wall in front of her. Fuck knew, that would scare her off fast as a goddamn jackrabbit.

I shot off a quick text, telling her I couldn't wait to see her.

She sent back a simple, **Same**, and my stomach relaxed enough, so I didn't go stomping into the office to tell the bitch behind the desk to kiss my ass.

I TIDIED up my cabin after mowing my mostly weed yard and hit the shower. Once in thin sweats and a t-shirt, I made sure to put on clean sheets, just in case.

An engine much too big to be Jill's car rumbled up the driveway, and I glanced out the front window to see Charley pulling up. Fucking butterflies made me feel like a damn kid again. I pulled open the door and stood on the top step.

He parked and hopped out, dressed in jeans and a nice shirt. Denim looked good on him. Hell, anything looked good on those powerful thighs. Add a nice button-down on top, his smooth jawline, and hawk-like nose... Everything about Charley pumped my blood straight to my dick.

"Everything okay?" I asked as he approached, checking me out as thoroughly as I did him.

"Yeah." He glanced at his watch. "Thought I was late."

"For?"

"Jill called. Said you invited us to dinner at six."

I snorted a laugh. "Sneaky little thing."

"She's not so little."

"She's fucking perfect."

He grinned, a curl of the lips I knew quite well. "That she is."

"Get your ass in here." I pushed open my door and strode back inside, the feel of Charley's gaze on my ass, giving me a boner. "Guess we're going to have that little talk."

Charley grabbed a couple of beers from the fridge while I pulled another plate from the cabinet, wanting to hide my tented sweats. He reached around me, setting my beer on the counter inches from my torso, the heat of him against my back, lighting my goddamn heart on fire.

"This'll cool ya off," he said against my ear and twisted to lean against the counter beside me.

"Fucker," I muttered, twisting the cap off and sucking down the cold brew.

He eyed my straining dick while adjusting his own. "How did we manage to hide this from each other for so goddamn long?"

I heaved an exhale and shifted to face him, deciding I didn't give a fuck if he knew how badly he made me ache. "I've loved you since the first time I saw you, Charley. I've always known, but I just didn't seem right."

"Because of what our parents taught us."

I nodded, holding his gaze.

"They're wrong."

"I know that now, but you have to know, two men openly together in this backward county will put bullseyes on our backs."

"Not all country boys hate gays."

"I'm not gay," I said. "Not interested in any dick but yours."

"Same."

That thought filled me with some sort of caveman bull-shit happiness. "So, where do we go from here?" I set my beer back on the counter, my fingers itching to touch him.

He set his aside, his eyes growing darker. "You could start by taking off your shirt."

"We only have a half-hour," I told him.

"More than enough time." Charley grasped my dick and yanked me against him.

So much for that shirt…

He claimed my mouth in a rough kiss, teeth scraping, the strength of him, his mouth, his hand on my length, the opposite of a woman's. Fuck, the taste of him … all man—harsh and taking, goddamn ball aching.

My head fucking reeled as I yanked at his jeans, hands fumbling with the button and zipper.

A deep groan echoed between our hungry mouths as my hand closed around his huge dick, and he yanked my sweats down, bringing our lengths together.

"Fuck." I tore my mouth off his and looked down between us, our hands clasping our dicks together. Pre-cum oozed from both of us, creating a slick, easy glide of wet heat between our skin.

"Christ, Kane." Charley hissed through his teeth, fucking along my length as I gave his hands control and dug my fingers into his hips, keeping him close. "I want to lose myself in you so goddamn bad."

My ass clenched at the thought, but I wanted it—badly. No lube… not enough time.

"Soon," I gasped out on the end of a moan, my balls drawing up and ready to fucking explode.

Charley lowered his head, seeking my mouth again, and I held on for fucking life as he claimed every piece of my heart I had left to give, every last centimeter he'd owned since fifth grade that I'd hidden away.

An ache swept through my entire goddamn body, so sweet, so searing, my eyes stung. Love—fucking unbridled, unleashed—let loose, and fucking soared through me. I came with a rush, Charley's grunts in tune with mine.

Our lips softened, more exploring than dominating and submitting as his hold on our dicks loosened. A shudder wracked through me, and I pulled back to look at him full in the face.

"The fuck was that?" I heard myself ask, even though I felt I knew.

"An appetizer."

We both laughed, and I stepped back, grabbing a roll of paper towels off the counter.

"Made a mess," I said, tossing one at the stripes of spunk up his nice shirt.

He ripped the damn thing off, and my mouth dried. Fuck,

he was one fine specimen of raw masculinity and power. Hot as hell—and he could be mine if I had the balls.

"What's on your mind, Kane?"

I tore my gaze off him and started toward my bedroom. "That you need to cover that shit up before I climb aboard and hump you like a goddamn dog."

"Hump away, boy."

I shot a glare over my shoulder. "I'm not your boy."

"You like my bossiness, though, don't you?" he asked with a smirk, following on my heels, his stare on my ass.

Fuck, yes. But I wouldn't ever admit to that shit. He'd have me on my knees every goddamn day... That thought had my dick swelling again, and I groaned, yanking my shirt drawer out from my dresser. I tossed him a t-shirt, loving the fact he would smell like my soap—like me.

I stripped out of my sweats, and he groaned from behind me.

"Been dreaming about that ass for years."

Those damn butterflies returned, and I bent deeper than I needed to pull out the bottom drawer.

"Fuck, Kane."

He grasped my hips, and wet heat slid up over my asshole. The fucker tongued me.

I grabbed hold of the dresser, my forehead on its top, and groaned, scared as fuck and turned on just as much. My dick swelled fully as he probed my ass with his tongue, swirling and poking where nothing had gone before.

Yeah, I wanted him. Desperately.

Charley licked up my crack and teased a fingertip through the saliva he'd left behind. "Let me in," he whispered, applying pressure.

I pushed against him, telling myself to relax like we'd always told whatever woman we'd had between us. His finger slid in, the burn curling my toes.

"Fuck, you're hot. Tight." Charley sounded as if he clenched his teeth, and I had to do the same as he worked his finger in deeper.

"Charley," I moaned as he rubbed against my prostate. "Fuck, that feels good."

"Imagine how good my dick will feel, buried inside your body."

Another moan rolled past my lips, and he pushed in another finger, stretching me so goddamn wide open, I bit my tongue to keep from whimpering.

"It'll feel better with lube," Charley said, but that goddamn stinging burn made my dick leak clear to the floor.

"Already feels good," I grunted.

He slid his fingers out and pushed back in, stealing my breath, bringing me up onto my toes.

"Fuck."

Charley stood, his hand working me, pressing his body against mine, the heat of his bare chest against my back like a furnace, breaking my skin out in goosebumps. His teeth found my earlobe, and he bit down hard enough, I gasped.

"This ass is mine. Don't give a fuck what people think, what they'll say, understand?"

I managed to nod, my balls tight and ready to explode as he rubbed along my prostate again.

"You're mine—but I'm willing to share with Jill if she wants us."

"Yes," I agreed without thought, already having decided, I wanted them both for as long as luck allowed.

"What I wanted to hear. Now, come for me." Charley bit down on my shoulder at the same time he shoved in a third finger, and I exploded, spunk flying from my dick without a touch to its straining length. I'd climaxed less than fifteen minutes earlier, but it seemed I hadn't in weeks.

Charley murmured his approval around his teeth's hold on my muscle, working my ass until one last shudder ripped through me.

"Good boy." He slid his fingers free, and I hissed at the sting he left behind.

"Fucker."

"Hopefully, soon," Charley said with a chuckle that went straight to my heart. "With me a mere membrane away from you."

"What if she wants to watch?" I asked, grabbing the closest piece of clothing I could find to wipe my cum off the dresser's front.

"Then I take your ass for the first time with our girl watching. Hell, I'll tell her to sit on your face while I fuck you."

"Gonna fuck me like a woman?"

"I want to look in your eyes the first time I take what belongs to me."

Fuck. That tone... I gave him my full attention. Stoic fucker stood ramrod straight, his dick at attention.

"Later."

I jerked my head up to find him smirking, his dark eyes full of lust even though they twinkled.

"You licked your lip."

"I didn't," I argued, not remembering doing so.

"I'll feed you my dick later, boy." Charley grabbed the

shirt I'd toss him off the floor while I growled a few curses over the new nickname.

"And what if *I* suddenly find my kink to bite?"

He pulled on the shirt, hiding the skin I wanted to explore with my fingers and tongue. "You bite my dick, and I'll shove it up your ass and give you a proper Deliverance-style ass fuck."

"I won't squeal like a pig," I stated as my ass clenched, and my dick considered twitching to life.

"We'll see about that." The fucker winked and left me standing there naked, weak in the knees, and full of emotions, I'd never expected to experience.

I'd given into Charley so damn easily, making myself vulnerable to a fuck by fate again. Loving meant losing. My stomach twisted, and I clenched my jaw against the familiar fear and anxiety of experiencing similar heartache. Reining in my mind and feelings the best I could, I yanked up another pair of pants, thin loungers that wouldn't hide jack shit from either Charley or Jill.

I glanced at my alarm clock—almost a quarter of seven.

"Fuck."

I pulled on a shirt and headed out of the bedroom.

JILL

I hoped Kane wouldn't be pissed at me for sending Charley up to his place early. When Charley had called me earlier in the afternoon, he told me he hadn't had a chance to speak with Kane.

While I certainly wanted more of their earth-shattering sexual attention, their laughter, and comfort I'd found in their presence, I couldn't help but continue to feel as though I didn't belong with them.

Kane and Charley had loved each other for years. They'd abstained, longed for, and probably suffered in silence. They deserved to be happy, and if I could help them find that path —together—I could step back, my heart hurting but mind at peace.

I left late, rolling up to Kane's cabin ten minutes after we'd agreed upon.

The door didn't open as I approached, so I peeked through the front window.

Oh, lordy...

Kane's bedroom door stood open at the cabin's back, and

Charley crowded him against his dresser, jean-clad legs against bare ones, Charley's forearm flexing as his hand worked, his upper body bent low over Kane's, hiding what he did.

Fire flared to life inside me as I realized what he did to Kane. Wetness welled inside my pussy, soaking through my panties within seconds, and I bit my lip to keep from moaning. Nipples beaded, and breath was lost.

I'd never seen such a hot sight.

Charley's arm stopped moving, and seconds later, he backed off.

Kane straightened but didn't fully turn, and I jerked away from the window, sitting my ass down on the top stair, my hands shaking while clutched the plastic container of salad I'd brought.

Holy hell. I gulped and fought to still my racing heart. They obviously had a *talk* of sorts, all right. *How long should I give them before knocking? Should I just drive off and hope they never know I showed up?*

I clenched my eyes shut, so damn torn, I didn't know what to do. Stay? Leave the two men to begin their lives together?

The front door opened, and I tensed.

"Hey."

Kane.

I forced a smile and angled toward him, sure my legs wouldn't yet hold me upright.

"How long you been here?"

"Long enough," I squeaked as heat flooded through me again.

He looked at the window, pink staining his cheeks when

he must have realized I'd seen quite the show. "Sorry about that."

"Don't apologize," I rushed to say, breathless as hell. "That was the hottest thing I've ever seen."

Charley filled the open doorway, drying his hands with a paper towel. "Hey, beautiful. I didn't even hear your car drive up."

Because your fingers were buried in Kane's ass. Heat fused my cheeks as he studied me.

He chuckled. "Guess I was kind of occupied."

"Yeah," I rasped out my agreement.

"Next time, you'll be on your knees, giving him something to focus on, so he doesn't shoot off like a green boy."

"Shut the fuck up, Woodhill," Kane muttered.

"Make me." Charley's eyes glinted with sexual aggression and enough hint, even I knew exactly how he wanted Kane to quiet his mouth.

"I-I think I'll leave," I whispered, forcing myself to stand on shaking legs, the salad bowl clutched tight against my stomach.

"Fuck, no." Charley took two quick steps, reaching for me, and I shied as he grasped my wrist. "Shit. Sorry." He dropped his hold like he'd burned me, and I shook my head, forcing my lungs to draw oxygen.

"No, it's okay."

He held out his hand, his gaze soft. "Stay with us."

"Only got two steaks, dipshit," Kane shot Charley's way while gently sliding his arm through mine and tugging me toward the front door. "You can have the rabbit food and bread."

"Fine by me," Charley said, falling in behind us. "I'll get my fill of meat later."

I choked on a laugh, and Kane shook his head, smiling.

"I'm going to go fire up the grill. Play nice," Kane said, releasing my arm. "You,"—he pointed at me—"get yourself a beer and relax. You,"—he pointed at Charley—"finish setting the table."

"Telling me what to do, boy?"

Kane growled something under his breath and strode out the cabin's back door, slamming it shut behind him. Charley and I eyed one another. At the waggle of his eyebrows, I burst into laughter, my nerves calming.

The second we sat down to eat, sexual tension zapped between all three of us. Kane set his attention on me. "Tell me about JD."

I glanced at Charley. "You told him?"

A muscle clenched in his jaw as he nodded. "Sorry, but I couldn't hold back everything, I told you I learned earlier today."

"No, it's okay." I steeled myself and turned back toward Kane. They both knew—no sense holding back any of the shit that had transformed me into the woman they'd come to know. I started with my parents' deaths, then JD's stepping in to comfort me, the signs I'd ignored, and the resulting insecurities I still fought to overcome from years of emotional and verbal abuse.

I am beautiful.

I am strong.

I am independent.

But the idea of leaning on two strong men tempted me to stay where I didn't belong.

While speaking, I saw the true extent of their love for one another. I'd helped them cross the barrier, holding them apart, and neither bothered to hide their feelings when I caught them staring at one another. The kind of love they obviously felt was storybook, the happily ever after I read about in my lusty male-on-male novels. Their love was also deeply rooted in their pasts.

I brought no value other than a good time. A needy, horny whore of a woman who didn't deserve one good man, let alone two.

"I don't belong here with you," I blurted out, pushing the last bit of steak along my plate, exhaustion from bringing all the shit of my life to light, weighing heavy on my shoulders. "This..." I glanced between the two of them, Kane's brow furrowing and Charley's face blank. "This is just for now," I rushed to say, my breathless voice betraying the restlessness in my chest and feet. "Okay?"

"Okay," Kane said a little too quickly.

Charley took his time before moving his stare off me toward Kane. He finally nodded, his face still an unreadable mask. "If that's what you want," he said, turning back toward me.

"Yeah." I swallowed. "It is." That wasn't what I wanted at all, but I knew better.

"So," Kane said, pushing to stand. "I've got s'mores stuff. Want to take this party outside?"

Moving slow, not jumping straight to fucking... I could deal with that, considering my emotional exhaustion. "Sure. Yeah."

"I'll build the fire," Kane said, glancing at Charley. "You do the dishes."

Charley made a tsking noise beneath his breath and muttered something about boys telling him what to do. Taking advantage of their choice to turn our conversation toward the silly, I agreed to help with the dishes.

"Gonna let me cop a feel while you're scrubbing, and I'm pretending to help?" Charley asked with a wink.

"Yes."

"Fuck," he groaned.

"How about you go build that fire, and I'll help do dishes?" Kane asked at our exchange, his lips twitching.

I bit my lower lip to keep from laughing while they studied one another, that rush of lust and tension rising in a flash. "How about you two boys go outside to build that fire —or put one out—and I'll clean up in here?"

Charley cocked an eyebrow Kane's way, infusing his cheeks with a luscious red.

Instant wetness sprang to life between my thighs. I would never tire of seeing them interact, never tire of their touch, their attention.

My heart ached as I reminded myself of the *just for now* law, I'd laid down. One day, I expected I would regret those words, but it was for the best. I'd helped them repair the bridge, helped bring them together, and it would have to be enough.

I was in fucking heaven, watching Kane pull Jill onto his lap, the second she joined us outside by the stone fire pit. He eyed me while gently kissing her neck as she settled against his back, her thighs spread across his.

Kane only had one lounge chair, but I made do with a cut log, elbows on my knees.

My gaze dropped to her little dress, riding high, and Kane widened his own thighs, pulling hers apart. It was too damn dark to see the heaven I hadn't nearly gotten my fill of.

"Kane," she whispered, her hands clasped atop his sprawled over her stomach.

"Hmm?" he hummed against her neck, turning his focus off me.

Her head tipped to the side, offering herself to him, her eyes on me as Kane nibbled and licked her sweet skin. The flames of the fire glinted off her golden skin, and the dampness Kane's kisses left behind on her neck. My dick swelled from the semi I'd been sporting since heading outside with

Kane. We'd kept to ourselves, discussing quietly what Jill had claimed to want.

Kane had been quick to agree to *just now* because he knew we could change her mind. I'd been slower to acknowledge what she wanted because it went against my instincts to demand she give into us, hold her close, and keep her safe. She hadn't shed one goddamn tear while telling us about her ex and all he'd done to tear her down.

She'd risen from the ashes a new woman, and I wanted nothing more than to watch her fly exactly as I'd claimed. I just didn't want her flying *away* from us.

"Pull up your dress, Jill," I murmured as the fire crackled between us. "Let me see what he does to you."

She bit her lower lip, her hands shaking as she obeyed me.

No. Fucking. Panties.

Her pink folds glistened in the fire's light.

"So fucking beautiful," I groaned and palmed my dick through my jeans. "Touch her, Kane."

He slid his hand down over her belly, middle finger parting her wet slit.

"She's wet," I stated, staring as he dipped his finger inside her pussy, causing her to lift her hips with a soft moan.

"Soaked," Kane replied, his nose buried beneath her ear. "For him or me?" he asked her.

"Both of you," she admitted, her gaze still latched on my face. "I want both of you."

I rounded the fire and dropped to my knees between their thighs, the heat warm against my back, but the low flames safe from tossing embers at me. Holding Jill's gaze, I leaned in and licked around Kane's finger, lazily pumping in and out of her pussy.

"Oh." She bit her lip, watching me.

"Let me taste her," I told Kane, and he pulled out his hand. I grasped his wrist and sucked his middle finger deep into my mouth, cleaning her creamy arousal off him. His groan pulled my balls up tight, painful inside my jeans. I let go of his finger with a pop and grabbed hold of the hard ridge along his left thigh.

"Fuck," he groaned as I squeezed harder and leaned in to lick Jill's pussy.

"Charley," she whispered, and I settled in to eat her out until she came all over my mouth, dripping onto my hand, working Kane beneath her. When she slumped against his chest, gasping for air, I sat back on my haunches.

"Take it out," I told Kane, pulling her forward toward his knees to give him access to his dick.

I kissed Jill's soft lips as her breathing slowed, drinking in her sweetness, her hungry tongue along mine lapping at her own taste, making me hard as fuck.

Kane's hands wrapped around her waist and tugged her back. He'd shoved his jeans to his knees and settled her down over his dick with one thrust.

Jill gasped, her back arching, and I dove back in, shoving his jeans to his ankles to widen his legs, licking her clit, trailing my tongue over Kane's length as he pulled out and shoved back in.

"Fuck, Charley." His rasped voice leaked pre-cum from my dick.

He tasted like her with hints of saltiness that could only be from him, like decadent chocolate and smooth peanut butter—the most divine flavor on the damn earth.

"Gonna come," Kane said through clenched teeth, and I

stood, pulling Jill up off him and into my arms. I wanted that spunk down Jill's throat when I claimed his ass.

"Inside. Now."

Jill clung to me, her pupils blown wide as I stood her at the foot of Kane's bed and stripped off her dress.

"Want to watch?" I whispered against her ear, and she gulped and nodded. Smirking, I pulled back and held her stare.

"On the middle of the bed, boy."

"Fuck you, Woodhill."

"Maybe next time."

Kane groaned, my own dick jerking at the thought of him inside my body, but I had something on my mind, something I wanted and planned to have.

He did as told, and I held his stare.

"Sit on his face, Jill. Give him something to focus on."

Her breasts swayed as she climbed onto the bed and lowered herself onto his face.

Kicking off my shoes and shoving down my jeans, I considered Kane's ass and the probable lack of lube. I had no issue making do—but he might.

I climbed onto the bed and spread his thighs, his groan and Jill's gasp over him, jerking my dick against the bed. "Touch your tits, little lady."

Lips parted, she did as told, and I shoved my face into Kane's ass, licking his puckered hole, the scent of his musk damn near rolling my eyes and seizing my nuts up tight. I lathed and probed, my hands grasping Kane's thighs to keep him still as he groaned against Jill's pussy.

Pre-cum leaked from me like a mother fucker. Sitting back on my haunches, I used the spit I'd left behind to lube my fingers. Kane grunted as I slid one finger in and cursed when I added a second, scissoring and readying his tight hole for my dick.

"Oh my God." Jill stared at my hand, working his dick, her hips gyrating, her fingers pinching her hard nipples. "That's so hot," she whispered.

Kane bucked beneath me, his heels planted on the bed, his own dick leaking.

I pulled my fingers from his ass, and he cursed again, but I crowded in close, so fucking reading to give him more.

Jill gasped, and I stilled, watching her while smearing my pre-cum down my length and lubing me up good for him.

"Going to come already?" I asked her, every inch of my skin on fire, with need to finally sink deep into his body.

"Y-yes," she groaned.

"Make her come, Kane."

Another deep groan left her lips, and she arched her back, crying out. The wet sounds of Kane lapping up her cum seized my balls tight against my body, and I grit my teeth, squeezing the base of my dick.

Jill slid off to the side, her hazed eyes peering up at me.

I turned my attention on Kane to find him watching me as well, dark lust filling his eyes.

"Do it," he said through clenched teeth, Jill's cream still smeared over his beard.

Moving forward, I held his stare, placing the tip of my dick against his ass. "Relax and let me in, Kane."

He pushed against me, and the head of my dick slid inside his tight heat.

"Holy fucking Christ," he hissed through clenched teeth,

his hands fisting the comforter, his asshole clenching tight around me.

"Shh," I murmured and pushed in more, my grip tight on his spread thighs.

"Fuck, Charley." He tipped his head back, the veins on his neck popping.

"Look at me."

He swallowed and met my gaze, the lust and pain in his eyes yanking against my restraint.

Jill slid closer and took his straining dick into her mouth.

"Fuck."

My little lady had read my mind, taking Kane mind off my abuse of his ass, I shoved in a few more inches, enough his body strangled my dick.

His chest rumbled, his eyes glazed by passion and pain.

A shift backward dragged my dick out halfway, and I flexed my hips, gaining another inch, pushing back in.

"All of it, Charley," Kane spit through clenched teeth. "I want it all."

I wanted it all—his body, his mind, his heart … his fucking soul.

Jill took him deep, and I thrust, burying balls deep in the man I'd loved for what seemed forever. Complete connection, a rush of overwhelming love and lust swelled inside me, thickening my throat as my balls rested against his body.

Love you...

Biting my lip, I eased out and thrust again, his grunt and curse spurring me on.

He twisted his hands in Jill's hair, and I gave over to my body's need to fuck, every slap of my balls against him, pushing a grunt past his lips. His eyes rolled back in his head.

"Give it to us, Kane," I growled at him, hanging on by a thread. *My love. My life.*

He bucked, his abs and pecs tensing, his ass clenching down on my dick. I gave him all I had, every spurt of cum in his ass seeming to carry a piece of my heart to his. I'd always wished to hold him so tight, I couldn't tell where one of us began and the other ended, but being inside of him, being one with him, outshone every dream, every fantasy I'd carried in my head.

He stilled at the same time I did, and Jill sat back, wiping his cum from the corner of her lip, glancing up at me with similar happiness on her face, I felt clear through to my toes. Her gaze dropped to where I was still buried inside Kane.

We belonged together. I could see the thought in her eyes, but did she include herself in that truth? Fuck knew, I did. Did Kane?

He laid like the dead, his face lax and eyes closed, a soft smile on his lips. That relaxed appearance faded the second I pulled out of his ass, a grimace and furrowed brow letting me know, it probably didn't feel as good as going in. I hoped to find out for myself—someday.

KANE

The intimacy I'd craved and my dreams had been fulfilled, and for the next two days, I couldn't think of anything else. Three big orders had come into the sawmill, keeping me and the other workers well past quitting time and leaving me exhausted. Too tired for much of anything but food and my bed, I contented myself with texting my two lovers every night.

Jill went to Charley's for dinner, and I once again encouraged them to enjoy themselves. I had every intention of rushing home to shower and getting my ass over to his place before the night ended, but five minutes before quitting time, Nat's bracelet caught on something at work and snapped. Beads flew in all directions, seizing my heart in my chest. Cursing, I scurried to grab up what beads I could find, my throat tight.

Nat...

That night came back with a rush, the bracelet clasped between my and Alana's hands as she breathed her last, Charley's name on her lips—not mine. We'd had one hell of a nasty fight a few hours earlier, and she'd taken off for her dad's in tears.

I'd been butt hurt over something so stupid, I couldn't even remember what she'd said. When I'd finally realized I'd been in the wrong, I climbed into my truck and drove through the driving rain, every flash of lightning creating a day-like atmosphere, the sky a bright backdrop against black trees and swaying branches. The booms of thunder had rumbled through my chest, and I couldn't drive fast enough to make things right.

I came upon Charley's truck on the side of the road, but it had been what his headlights illuminated that stole my breath and stalled my heart.

Crushed metal. Shattered glass. A car bent beyond recognition.

I knew the man next to what was left of the driver's side door.

"Fuck. Nat…" I whispered, standing and staring at the tiny beads in my shaking palm. Not even half of them, not nearly enough to remake the bracelet I hadn't removed since restringing it the day I'd buried my wife and daughter.

Grief slammed into me, and I clenched my teeth to keep from sobbing.

I left work without a backward glance, not giving two shits, my boss hollered after me, asking where I was going. Zero fucks left to give when it came to her and the mill.

Twenty minutes later, I sank to the ground beside their tombstones, my shoulders slumped, tears streaming down my cheeks.

"I'm so sorry," I told Alana, my fingers tracing the carving of her name in cold stone. "It was my fault you were upset. My fault you were driving. I never apologized." I raised my eyes to the cloudy sky overhead, hoping to hear her voice. A whisper in the wind picked up, swaying the trees overhead in a slight rustle of leaves. I fucking needed something—anything to let me know she heard and forgave, but as with every time I listened for her, disappointment ended up twisting my stomach.

Alana was gone. My sweet daughter was gone.

I had the only person whose blessing over my moving on mattered—Charley's—so why did my heart still ache with the need to know Alana wanted the same for me?

Darkness crept across the sky along with the scent of incoming rain and silence, except for a few birds, still filled my ears. Memories ran through my head as though I relived my life with them. From watching Alana walk down the aisle to Nat being laid on her chest after she came shrieking into the world.

I laughed, tears coursing down my cheeks.

Nat's first smile, Alana's and my joy, watching her take her first steps. Walks to watch the sunset—her hot breath on my ear that had always sent tingles to my toes.

Scrubbing a hand down over my face, I let out a heavy exhale. "I loved you more than anything—both of you."

But I love Charley, too. Maybe even Jill...

My emotions depleted, I pushed up off the ground.

"If you can hear me," I whispered, "I love you still. You both own a part of my heart, but I realize now, there's still a part left. I want to live, Alana. I don't want to be alone and heartbroken anymore. If my being with Charley and possibly Jill doesn't sit well with you, if you can't stand the thought of us sharing a bed every night for the rest of my life, let me know." I swallowed hard. "Please," I whispered.

The breeze kicked up, a gust suddenly swaying the nearby maple, turning its leaves upside down. I glanced westward behind me, the looming clouds clenching my gut. A low rumble of distant thunder tightened every muscle in my body. I was a half-hour from home, which lay to the west. No way would I make it back before the storm hit me head-on.

Another storm for me to face alone...

But I didn't have to. I hurried to my truck, grabbed up my cell of the console, and called Charley.

"I need you," I managed to rasp out past the tightness of panic in my throat.

"Where are you?" All business, his tone hinted at strength I needed to lean on.

"The cemetery."

"Can you make it here before the rain hits, or do you want me to come get you?"

I glanced toward the clearer sky in the east and once more at the looming clouds behind me in my rearview as a streak of lightning zoomed across the sky. *Fuck.*

"I'll be there in ten."

My heart raced in my chest, but I forced myself to keep to a decent speed as I headed eastward. Every crack of thunder winced my shoulders and face, memories flashing as quickly as the sky lit around me. It took me nine long as fucking minutes to pull onto Charley's driveway. The first drops of rain hit my windshield as I put my truck in park.

He stood on the farmer's porch, eyeing the clouds. The second I hopped out into the wind, the damn sky opened up, dumping atop my head. Lightning flashed, illuminating his dark gaze, and the thunder crashed as I raced straight into his arms.

"Got you," he mumbled, pulling me deeper under the roof as the storm raged around us.

"Don't ever let go." I clung to him, my eyes clenched shut, my entire body trembling.

"Not gonna. Now, let's get our asses inside and get you in the shower. You fucking stink."

With shaky laughter, I stepped out of Charley's arms into his house.

"NAT'S BRACELET BROKE AT WORK," I told him an hour later as we sat nursing beers, the storm gone, the scent of rain and wet earth heavy in the cool breeze he allowed through opened windows. "I lost my shit. Took off." I swigged my beer and picked at the label. "Probably don't have a job to go back to, but I don't give a shit." I tipped my head back against his couch and closed my eyes, breathing in the scent of ozone with the underlying sandalwood from his soap I'd used. "I'm so fucking tired."

"Come on." Charley grasped my hand and pulled me up. "You can stay with me tonight."

My dick twitched at the thought of having him all to myself, but I smelled Jill's perfume on the pillow I hugged the second I collapsed on his bed.

"She was here last night," Charley said as I sniffed her deep into my lungs.

"Did you fuck her?"

"Yes."

I let out a sigh and curled in on myself. "I thought I lost you when I lost Alana," I told him as he flicked off the lights.

The bed dipped behind me, and I scooted closer to the center of the bed giving him room. Charley wrapped his arms around me, his cheek against the back of my head.

"You'll never lose me," he murmured, lacing his fingers through mine.

He slid one of his legs between mine, and I shifted back against his groin. He sported a semi but made no move to hump my ass, simply held me. He kept me from being lonely and gave my body the physical touch it craved. He was made up of sinew and hard muscle, and a part of me craved soft sweetness, more of the woman whose scent filled my nose.

"I've only just met Jill, but she fills up a part of me that's been missing," I told him the truth in my heart, while guilt admitting it to the man who'd fallen for me, who possibly loved me, slid in to churn my stomach.

"It's okay."

"I don't feel like it is."

Charley squeezed my fingers. "Alana would want you happy. If that's Jill, then that's what I want for you, too."

"If I want you both?" I asked, my heart in my throat.

"I've always wanted you, Kane. Always will." His hot breath warmed my ear, sending a tingle down my spine. "I love you. That won't change or stop until I'm dead and buried, or longer if there's an afterlife. But I want her, too, and if there's a chance to make it work, I'll do whatever I have to do."

"People won't accept it."

"Don't give a fuck." He squeezed my fingers again. "Let them gossip. Let them spew hatred in their closed-minded bigotry. You're a part of me, I'm tired of living without. Fucking exhausted."

I rolled, pressing tight against his front.

"I don't want to hide away anymore," he whispered as I brushed my nose against his. "I want to be your shoulder. Your rock. I want to hold your hand through life's storms, facing them together."

"I love you," I whispered across his lips with my own.

With a groan, Charley grasped my ass and pulled me impossibly tight against him, sealing his mouth over mine. I'd expected dominance, rough and hot, but he tasted, taking his time, and seemed to suck my soul from my mouth.

We hardened and ground against one another, and the second I told him I wanted him, he left me alone, grasping at the sheets. The lights flared to life overhead, and I peered after his stalking form as he crossed the room, opened the bed stand, and pulled out a bottle of lube. He dripped it down my length and worked me until my balls drew up tight.

"You feel so fucking good," I told him through grit teeth.

"This'll feel even better." He climbed atop me and positioned my dick against his asshole.

"Charley—"

"Shh." He lowered himself, and as his tight heat clamped around the head of my dick, my damn eyes rolled back into my head.

"Fucking *hell.*"

He impaled himself with one slow descent, and I grasped his thighs, my eyelids jerking open as he bottomed out against my groin.

He lifted and lowered without a goddamn wince, and I

packed almost as much length and girth as his dick dripping onto my abs.

"How'd you manage that," I gasped as he repeated the motion.

"Fantasized about having you this way for a long fucking time, Kane. I might have gotten a toy or two."

"How'd they work out for ya?" I tossed out, trying to keep my mind from giving way to my balls' need to explode.

He chuckled and leaned down to plank over me, his dark eyes capturing me, his ass squeezing the hell out of my dick. "Pretty damn well, I'd say. What do you think?"

"I think you feel fucking amazing."

"Mmm." Charley stole my mouth and made love to me, rocking until I couldn't hold back, until we both grunted our release, his cum smearing between our bellies.

Fucking *life*, save for one little piece of heaven.

JILL

It poured into the early morning hours on Friday, and the humidity settled in long after the clouds passed. A shipment of groceries arrived with the sun, so I helped Annette unpack them and stock the shelves.

At every engine rumble, I glanced out the front window, hoping to see Charley or Kane's trucks. Neither arrived by their usual work time, and I fought off disappointment. I missed Kane. Hadn't seen him all week, and even though I'd gotten my fill of Charley—literally—almost every night since the weekend, I felt something lacked.

Kane.

I missed him behind me when Charley cuddled me against his chest, both our bodies satiated and relaxed. I missed his rasped tenor, his whispered words against my neck. I missed hearing his heartbeat beneath my ear.

"You look like you're pining away over there."

Face heating, I turned to find Annette a few feet away at the aisle's end. She'd taken off her light sweater and wore a sleeveless top, baring her arms for the first time I'd seen.

Crisscrossed scars ran up the outside of her arm, disappearing beneath her shirt.

"Pretty, aren't they?" she asked, raising her arm when she noted where I stared.

"What happened?" I set the can of beans I had in hand on the shelf.

"I had a beau before Roy." Annette dropped her arm and returned to her work, stacking single packages of toilet paper. "He reeled me in with sweet words, but it turned out he wasn't so sweet."

That sounded familiar...

"I stayed too long and paid a horrible price."

"I'm sorry," I whispered as I felt my spirit align with hers in shared pain.

"Roy knew about my scars, those inside and out, and loved me still." Another two rolls found their way atop the pyramid she built before she continued. "It's been sixty years of not-always bliss, but I wouldn't trade my life for anything. I also wouldn't change the past. It led me here, to Roy. Same as yours did for you, Jill."

I chewed the inside of my lip and finished shelving the box of beans, Annette's stare on my face enough to singe.

"Those two men love you, too."

My hair whipped as I jerked toward her. "What? Why would you think that?"

"They both look at you like Roy does me, like I'm the stars in the night sky, the rays of sun after a storm."

Mind blown—and blank—I worked my mouth, not capable of speaking. She thought they loved me, but she'd said *too* as though she thought I loved *them*.

"They're good boys, who sowed their wild oats back in

the day, but maybe I was wrong to think what they desired in their lives was mere child's play. Some people around these parts might not like what you three have going on, but if Charley and Kane are what make you happy..." Annette shrugged. "Not anyone's business but yours."

I nodded absently, stewing over her words. We finished stocking between the two customers who meandered in, looking for bait, then I headed upstairs to grab some lunch at her insistence.

Charley had set up a group text to include me and Kane and sent a dinner at his house invite for that night. Kane had already replied he'd be there, and the butterflies erupted in my stomach.

Me: **I'll bring the bunny food.**

Kane: **Just bring yourself. Don't need that shit.**

Charley: **I like the bunny food—but I like the taste of you better.**

Oh, Lordy. Arousal sprang to life, thinking about his clean-shaven jaw and those teeth marking the insides of my thighs.

Me: **I like it when you taste me.**

Kane: **Damnit, you two, I'm trying to work over here.**

I giggled, but footfalls on my stairs cut me short. Brow furrowed, I hurried to the window and peeked out.

Annette climbed the stairs, grasping my rail, her face pale.

I yanked the door open. "Everything okay?"

Lips pursed, she nodded and shooed me back inside.

"What's going on?" I asked, wrapping my arms around my middle and stepping into my tiny kitchen.

"A man stopped by a few minutes ago." She studied my face as I felt mine pale the same as hers. "He was asking about you. Showed me a picture, but I barely recognized you."

"I-I've changed quite a bit in the past six months," I managed to say past the sudden tightness in my throat and the instant quaking in my stomach. "What did you tell him?"

"Seeing as how he looked like he was up to no good, I denied knowing you."

"H-he left?"

"He did." She peered at me as I fought for calm. "There something I need to know, Jill?"

Her tender voice sprang tears to my eyes. "Ex-husband," I whispered. "He wasn't a kind man, either."

"So, that's what brought you up here from Maryland?"

I nodded, swallowing against the lunch I'd downed, threatening to heave back up.

"Do your boys know about him? That he's looking for you?"

"They know." I shifted, eyeing the door.

"Stay, Jill," Annette stated gently as though she felt the sudden itch in my feet to run and never stop. "You're strong enough on your own, but let those boys be your rock. Let them help protect you if need be."

Tears slid down my cheeks, and I hugged myself tighter.

"You can't keep running. You've got a new life here, you've found love again."

Love? I wasn't so sure. "But what if I'm not ready?"

"You won't know unless you dive in headfirst."

"That's what I did with JD and look where it took me."

"Yes." Annette smiled and patted my arm. "Look where it brought you."

A shuddered breath sagged my shoulders. "I-I should call Charley."

"Yes, you should. Tell him JD is driving a black SUV of sorts. Didn't catch the license plate, but I'm pretty sure it was a Ford. One of the big ones like you see in motorcades."

He still had the Expedition. I'd always thought he liked big vehicles to make up for his pencil dick. I'd definitely upgraded... I bit back a giggle and swiped my eyes with the backs of my hands.

"Thank you, Annette."

She pulled me into a tight hug, and I smiled, breathing in the scent of mothballs and the ancient Avon perfume Roy loved.

"Go on now." She patted my arm again and stepped back. "Call your boys, then take the rest of the day off."

I helped Annette down the stairs, then hurried back up, dialing Charley as I went.

He didn't answer, and my itching feet had me scanning the tiny apartment, temptation to pack my bags and take off, churning my stomach again.

CHARLEY

Sweat plastered my t-shirt to my back, and my muscles strained from carrying my corner of the stretcher, holding the injured hiker, but I couldn't be happier. Thoughts of Kane and Jill filled my mind as we grunted with exertion to get the man off the mountain.

Dappled sunlight played across the forest floor, dancing over roots and rocks as though showing me where to place my feet. Fate leading me, I considered. Same as my whole life, waiting for the right time to bless me with what I'd always dreamed of having—my love and a woman to share him with. She was a gift herself and had found her way into my heart, but love? I couldn't tell. Couldn't decide, but I knew I wanted her to stay in my life alongside Kane.

I'd never known such contentment, and hope, things would only get better, kept my footsteps light beneath the weight of the obese man.

Until we reached the dirt lot where an ambulance waited to cart the hiker off, my muscles strained, exhaustion like I hadn't known since my days in the army weakening my legs.

I climbed into my truck once the situation had been settled and let out a huge groaned exhale. A quick call into dispatch filled them in on the situation, and I finally got a chance to grab my cell.

Jill had tried calling ten minutes earlier. Just the sight of her name on my screen, sweet little lady, made me forget my exhaustion. Grinning, I dialed her back.

"Charley."

My smile disappeared at the tone of her voice. "What's wrong?"

"JD … Annette said he was here looking for me. Black SUV."

I cranked the engine over and pulled out of the lot, dirt and stones flying from beneath my tires. A flick of my fingers turned the emergency lights on. "You okay?"

She didn't answer, and my heart rate kicked up to speed with my truck.

"Don't run, Jill. Don't you leave me … us. Talk to me."

"I-I'm scared, Charley." Her voice shook, the hint of tears and panic lacing her words backing up her claim.

I raced down the two-lane road, flying past a car that pulled onto the berm to get out of my way. "Did you call Kane?"

"He's not answering either."

"Get in your car and get up the mountain to him. I'll be there in fifteen minutes."

"I'm *scared*, Charley," she repeated with a whisper, and my chest ached at the smallness of her voice, the thought of her taking off like an awl taken straight to my rapidly beating heart.

"You're strong, Jill. You can do this."

A sob came through loud and clear over the line, clenching my stomach. She was going to fucking run—I just knew it. *Fuck.*

"Stay put. Don't open your apartment door for anyone but me or Kane, understand? Don't go anywhere. Let us help you. Please."

"O-okay." Timid mouse … what happened to my sassy woman who'd grown a pair?

"I'm on my way, Jill. I won't let anything happen to you," I swore on my goddamn life. Fate wasn't going to fuck with me this time.

She sniffled in my ear as I sped past another slow granny. "Hurry."

I hung up and dialed Kane.

No answer. He didn't have the sawmill job anymore and had left my bed that morning to work on a table he'd been building. Five minutes up the damn road from Jill and he couldn't be reached.

Cursing, I clutched the steering wheel, eyeing the dark clouds of a storm rolling in.

Don't you fucking dare. Don't even...

Adrenaline kept me focused, and I forced myself to breathe evenly, slowly. Calm descended, but I didn't let up on the gas, the truck's siren muffled.

I'd lost my sister and lost the man I loved because of it. I wouldn't lose Jill, and I refused to lose my second chance with Kane.

JD Walters didn't have a record, no back taxes, nothing shady—not even a goddamn speeding ticket. Squeaky clean, the type of man who couldn't be touched without evidence. Flattening his nose wouldn't be an option. Neither would putting a bullet through his brain. He'd hurt Jill, and I wanted him to suffer, but I would need to find a way to make it happen without hurting myself or my loved ones in the aftermath.

The Mountain View Store appeared around the corner, and I slowed to pull in, some of the tension leaving my shoulders at the sight of Jill's car out back. Before I slammed the truck into park, she flung open her door and raced down the stairs.

I hopped from my truck and caught her in my arms, her sobs muffled against my neck as I quickly scanned the lot and cabins along the woods. No black SUV to be seen.

"I got you, little lady. No one is ever going to hurt you again." I whispered assurances against her ear, walking around to the passenger door as she clung to me.

"I need you to get in the truck."

Jill released her hold, sniffing, and her red-rimmed eyes clenched my stomach all over again.

Annette opened the store's back screen door, her wrinkled lips pressed in a thin line.

"I'm taking her out of here," I called out, rounding the front of my truck.

"Hide her away, Charley. I didn't trust the looks of that man. He means her no good."

"He won't ever touch her again. I'll make sure of it."

Her gaze softened. "Between you and Kane, I have no doubt she'll be safe."

"She will be."

"She belongs with the two of you."

I paused in pulling open the driver's door, eyeing the woman who knew too much about too many damn people.

"Give her the love and respect she deserves." Annette's stink eye promised I'd reap the consequences if we didn't.

"Will do, ma'am."

"Don't ma'am me. Get our girl out of here and don't bring her back until it's safe. Roy and I will make do. We always have."

I nodded and climbed in, casting a quick glance at Jill. She hugged her knees up tight against her chest, tear tracks lining her cheeks. Afraid she would shy away from any aggressive move I made to yank her onto my lap and kiss her fear away, I kept my hands to myself.

A call came through from dispatch halfway up Kane's driveway. A rattlesnake had made itself comfortable in someone's garage, and I was the closest Warden.

"En route," I told dispatch, my face and heart hard. Fucking timing... I hung up and cursed while pulling in front of Kane's cabin.

He sauntered out of the woodshop, brushing sawdust off his hair, a goofy grin on his face. His lips flatlined the second I hopped out of the truck, my face still hard as stone. Before I rounded the front, Jill did the same and ran, throwing herself into his arms.

The sobs started back up, and he glared at me while holding her tight.

"The fuck?" he mouthed at me.

"JD's in town and looking for her," I said, my voice low, my growing rage barely held in check.

Thunder rumbled far off to the west.

"Fuck." Kane closed his eyes and held her tighter, kissing the top of her head. "Gonna be okay, Jill. Not going to let that fucker hurt you."

"I got a call from dispatch." I clenched my fists at my sides, my stomach churning. "Can't stay."

Kane met my steady gaze. "Get your ass over here for five fucking seconds, would you?" he rasped, his voice unsteady, and I cursed the sky threatening to shred his insides.

My throat tightened, and three strides took me to my lovers. I wrapped my arms around them both, touching my nose first to Kane's then to the back of Jill's head.

Heaven in a hellish situation.

I inhaled until it hurt, then slowly let it leak out of my lungs, eyes closed. "Keep her safe for us, Kane." I had to force myself to step away, and the second I turned, Jill threw her arms around me from behind.

"Thank you."

I clasped my hand over hers atop my chest, glancing over my shoulder to find Kane hugging her back. His fist settled on my shoulder.

Fucking *heaven*.

"I'd give my life for you," I managed past that damn swelling in my throat. "Both of you."

Turning my truck around, I couldn't bear to look back at them. Otherwise, I'd never leave, and I'd end up in trouble with the Game Commission.

I trusted Kane to watch over her, even if his PTSD threatened otherwise.

KANE

The first day of running my own business and the shit hit the fan. Add in the distant thunder, and my stomach tied in fucking knots.

"I tried calling you." Jill clutched the arms I'd wrapped around her middle, the second Charley walked to his truck, her body trembling against my front.

"Shit. Sorry. Must have left my cell in the house when I went in for lunch."

Charley disappeared around the switchback, and I turned Jill, so I could see her face.

"You okay?" I brushed the hair off her forehead, the sight of her red, puffy eyes a kick to my gut.

"I-I will be." She rubbed her lips together and tried for a smile. "I think."

Fuck, this woman... At that moment, I realized I'd become emotionally involved to the point where living without Jill would suck major ass. The thought of her being taken away from me, from Charley, made me want to smash the shit out of something with my hammer.

"Come on in." I tried for a smile, hating the tremors the impeding storm roiled in my limbs. "I'll get you something to drink."

"Got any whiskey?"

"Just beer."

"That'll have to do."

I tugged her under my shoulder and led her into the house, locking it up good and tight behind us. The storm moved in as we sat on my couch with our beers, my cell on the table next to my revolver—just in case. Jill simply nodded, and at that moment, I knew JD was beyond a rotten bastard.

She told me what Annette had told her, and her body's natural reaction to fold in on itself kept my focus off the darkening sky outside the cabin's windows. When she finished, I set our drinks aside and pulled her onto my lap, cradling her face in my hands. She hadn't held back voicing her emotional response, I could see without her telling me and felt I owed her the same vulnerability as lightning lit the window behind her.

"Storms bring back the night of Alana and Nat's deaths."

Her eyes filled with empathy, and she leaned in to gently brush her lips over mine. "What can I do to help make it better?"

"You could kiss me again," I said with a crooked smirk, already distracted from the nearing storm by her sweet ass on my thighs and hints of perfume.

Her smile faded, the heat in her eyes swelling my dick to life. She kissed me again without the gentleness of the first. Groaning, I wrapped my hands in her hair, drinking her deep into my lungs, losing myself in her lips, the taste of her tongue, and her sweet breath, laced with hops.

I'd never had a woman in my bed—and I wanted Jill laid out for my feasting—alone, just the two of us. Pushing to my feet, I grasped her ass to keep her in my arms, our mouths still fused. I made it to the bedroom, only bumping against one chair in my lust-filled rush.

In two minutes flat, I had her on her back, naked, and staring up at me with enough lust to leak pre-cum from the dick I held in my hand. Her nipples beaded beneath my stare, her taut stomach shivering as I slid my gaze down over her long torso.

"Spread your legs for me," I murmured, my gaze dropping to the trimmed patch of dark curls and the peek of her pink nub. "Let me see how perfect you are."

She slid her thighs apart, her pussy lips pulling away from each other, revealing the wetness inside. Drool coated my mouth at the memory of her taste, and I dropped my dick to climb between her thighs and bury my tongue and nose against her wet warmth.

"Oh God," Jill gasped and grasped my head, her thighs clenching against my ears.

My dick jerked, and I humped the mattress while licking and sucking every inch of her pussy—fucking divine, like the sweetest honey.

"Need you," she whimpered, tugging my hair. Licking up her slit, I flicked her clit a few times before sliding up over her body, tasting what skin I could get my mouth on before she had me where she wanted me. Notched against her opening, our breaths held.

Same as the first time I'd been inside her body, I cradled

her face in my hands, holding her gaze. It was my turn to sink into *her*, burying my dick deep against her womb. We muttered curses, mine over the velvety wetness clenching at my length and sucking me in deeper.

"You're perfect, Jill," I murmured and leaned down to take her mouth, my lips hungry, my tongue desperate to taste more of her. Her arousal coated my length, dripping down on my drawn-up balls, creating a slick mess for every grind of my pelvis against hers.

"So fucking good," I whispered against her mouth and flexed my ass harder, claiming that last inch.

Jill gasped against my mouth, and I pulled back, that delicious drag enough to roll my eyes back into my head.

Thunder crashed, but I barely heard as I thrust deep against her womb again.

"Kane..." Jill arched beneath me, ripping her mouth away to pant and whimper.

I lifted onto my hands in a plank, watching her face. Watching as she watched my dick slide back into her willing body. Absolute perfection. I felt myself fall harder as she grasped my shoulders, pulling me back down against her sweat-slickened chest. Our mouths fused, and I swore lightning struck, pounding my heart and setting off fireworks in my brain.

Jill moaned, then gasped.

I thrust harder, deeper, sliding her body along my mattress until her head rested against the headboard. Couldn't get deep enough. Couldn't seem to bury my soul deeply into hers, losing myself in everything she was.

"Going to come," she panted between thrusts, seizing my balls, and I lifted once more to latch my gaze onto hers.

"Come all over my dick, baby. I want to feel you sucking me deeper."

Her breath caught, and she arched. "Kane … oh, shit!"

Wetness seeped around my dick, soaking my balls and the bed beneath, spurring my hips onward as if they had a mind of their own. Her final tremor sent a rush of cum up through my shaft, erupting against her womb, and I pressed harder, digging my toes into the bed, desperate to go deeper. I wanted to burrow forever inside her heart, her mind, where she'd never be able to rid herself of me.

"Kane..." she groaned as I thrust again, grunting with my own release.

"Christ, Jill." I captured her mouth, my entire body jerking with the final spurt, depleting my energy straight to fucking zero. Elbows on the bed, I collapsed against her chest, holding her face in my hands, kissing her soft, parted lips, along her narrow jaw to the soft skin beneath her ear.

She shuddered beneath me and let out a sigh, her hands soothing down the muscles along my spine.

Thunder rumbled, and I lifted as a shiver licked over me. I became aware of the rain pounding on my metal roof but focused on Jill's chestnut-colored fathomless eyes, full of unnamed emotion I felt tugging on my own heart.

"Okay?" I whispered and kissed her lips again.

"Mmm," she murmured her reply into my mouth.

I wrapped my arms around her and rolled, carrying us to the edge of my queen-sized bed, keeping my dick firmly planted inside her body.

She settled in with a smile, squeezing her inner walls around me, toying with my beard. "Has anyone told you that you're beautiful?"

Snorting a laugh, I shook my head.

"You are." Tracing my lips with her fingertip, she pulled on the lower, parting my lips. "You've got a sexy mouth. I like it."

"I like you."

Her smile faded, raising an alarm in my heart. "I like you, too," she whispered, easing the rising anxiety inside me.

"Come here." I pulled her head down against my shoulder, closing my eyes, soaking in the softness, the warmth of her body atop mine. While I wouldn't have minded Charley's heater-like presence beside us, his hands and mouth on both of us, I took comfort in what Jill had offered to take my mind off the storm—her body, but perhaps a bit of her heart as well.

CHARLEY TEXTED over a dozen times to check on us until he showed up at five-fifteen. I expected he would need help calming the fuck down. Tension rode his shoulders as he sat down to dinner with us, his face stoic as fuck, his brow furrowed.

"What'd you find out?" I asked before cutting into the chicken I'd grilled.

"I've been asking around. He's at a motel near Renovo, according to the owner, and he told JD he'd seen you." Charley glanced at Jill.

Lips pursed, she nodded and took her time slicing off a bite of chicken. "Moonlight Motel?"

"Yes."

"I stayed there for a week before finding that *Help Wanted* sign in Annette and Roy's window."

"Think he'll just move on when he comes up empty?" I asked, glancing between the two.

"He's a bloodhound," Jill whispered. "A pit bull."

I shoved a bite in my mouth and chewed, eyeing Charley as he studied Jill, his brow's furrow easing as emotion flickered in his eyes. The fucker was falling for her—no doubt. He'd had her in his bed alone more than I had, and it had only taken the one time of our bodies and souls connecting for me to know, I was a damn goner for the woman.

"Since Kane's working from home now, I would like for you to stay here with him."

Jill jerked her head toward Charley. "What about you? Will you stay with us, too?"

Charley smirked at me. "No offense, but this place is kinda small."

"Never expected to get involved again," I said. "Didn't want to."

"And now?" he asked, studying my face, his voice low.

"I'm involved. Heavily." I eyed both my lovers one at a time. "Happily."

"I'm tired of fighting this, Kane," Charley said.

"So, don't. I'm too tired to give a shit what people say."

"So am I."

Our gazes latched as pure fucking euphoria swept through me.

In my periphery, Jill sat back in her chair as though wanting to slide beneath the table and disappear.

I tore my gaze off Charley's dark eyes and caught hers.

Pain replaced the emotions, the happiness I'd basked in while she'd sat on my dick a few hours earlier. "Feet itchy?"

She frowned at me.

"Don't even think about it," Charley muttered, his voice rumbling his chest.

I grasped her hand to keep her from running. "You belong to us."

Her chin lifted with defiance that twitched my dick, glinting in her eyes. "I belong to no man."

"How about *two* men?" Charley waggled his eyebrows. "I'll bite you, mark you, so everyone knows you're Kane's and mine."

"The hell you will," she muttered although her pupils swelled.

"Jill."

She turned toward me.

"Only stay if it's what *you* want," I said. "We're not asking to own you, the way JD did. You'll have your independence to come and go as you please."

Her eyes softened, although the lust remained.

"As long as you're in our bed every night," Charley added, his no-nonsense tone not open for argument.

Jill's lips twitched as though a smile begged to release. "Kane's bed isn't big enough for the three of us."

"Then we'll replace it with mine."

"It's kinda small in here," I reminded him, my heart damn near in my throat from sheer fucking joy.

"Then we put on an addition," Charley said as though it was no big deal. "I've got my inheritance, and I'll sell Mom and Dad's house. We'll turn this place into one of those log houses they show on TV."

Although he stated his idea with assurance, a hint of unease lay in his eyes. Wariness? Fear of losing us? Fuck knew, that same fear lingered in my head, but I wanted it, was willing to be vulnerable and put my heart out to be squashed again. Charley was worth it. Jill was worth it.

"If you're sure that's what you want," I said, my voice rising at the end as though a question.

Lips tight, he nodded, his eyes shutting down into Charley mode and make me question his affirmative answer.

"So, does this mean we're like … a thing?" Jill asked. "Seeing each other? All three of us?"

"Fucking right." Charley shoved chicken in his mouth and grinned, but I'd known him long enough to note the line at the corner of his mouth. Wherever the unease stemmed from, it was buried deep—and worsened my own fear.

I squeezed Jill's hand, allowing Charley privacy for the time being. "Will you stay?"

She let out a slow exhale, glancing between the two of us. "If fate allows it."

Fate would fucking allow it, or I was going to have a serious screaming match with the skies the next time they opened up.

If I could find the balls to do so.

I shifted on my chair, my own unease suddenly eating at my guts. We just needed to keep Jill safe until her ex went looking elsewhere. I wouldn't consider a different outcome.

We attempted sex in Kane's bed. Charley ended up falling to the floor, and I laughed my ass off, feeling free as hell, even though the threat of JD lay very real in the back of my head. An hour later, Kane and I followed Charley to his house after stopping by my apartment for my stuff.

Charley explained to Annette, I would be staying with him at his house while Kane helped me pack up my meager belongings. She met me at the bottom of the stairs in her robe and slippers, holding her arms wide. I sank into her soft embrace, the scent of mothballs bringing tears to my eyes.

"Take as long as you need, child, and if that means for good, you just let me know. Don't worry about me and Roy. We'll make do and find someone else to help out around here if that's what you need."

Tears prickled my eyelids, and I nodded, unable to speak.

"Don't stop rising from those ashes," Annette whispered and patted my cheek. "You've come this far. Don't let anything stop you."

Throat tight, I hopped in my car and followed Charley out of the parking lot, Kane's truck behind me.

I drove in silence, fighting to focus on the sweet sting between my thighs from having both men at once rather than the upheaval, my life once more experienced. Would JD's inability to let me go ever end? I couldn't imagine that being so unless one of us rotted in the ground, and with the two men I'd just found, I didn't want it to be me.

The ache in my core felt too good—addictive.

They wanted me to stay with them, but I still felt like an intruder, unworthy of their attention and affection. What woman wanted two men instead of the normal one?

Whore.

I swallowed against the rising anxiety over JD's voice in my head, my skin crawling and feet itching. If not boxed in by trucks, I would have been tempted to take the next turn and never look back.

Annette suggested I let them help protect me. Both men asked for the same.

Could I trust them? The determination to stand on my own, that independent spirit I'd searched for and had begun to recognize inside myself, kept me from doing so fully. My stomach in knots and adrenaline keeping me on edge, I parked alongside Charley's truck.

Silence filled my car's interior, my breaths loud in the stillness.

I am beautiful.

I am independent.

I am strong.

My desire to own all three flooded through me at the chanted affirmations in my head and heart, but perhaps being strong meant knowing when to let go and allow others to help.

Charley and Kane both approached my driver's door when I didn't get out, and I peered at them through the window. An ache spread through my chest as the floodlights on Charley's farmer's porch lit their faces.

My head might hold back from trusting and wanting, but my heart couldn't. Like magnets, they drew me out of the car and into their waiting arms, and I went willingly, recognizing strength didn't always mean standing on your own two feet.

EVERY MORNING, Charley went into work while Kane and I went back to his place. A borrowed laptop from Charley allowed me to help Kane set up a website while he worked in his shop, creating furniture to sell. I took dozens of pictures of the pieces in his home, deciding which angles and lighting worked to best showcase his work.

Every night, the three of us crawled into Charley's bed, with me in the middle, but sometimes I ended up on the outskirts, watching the two men together, pleasuring myself to the sight of them losing themselves in one another. Each and every fantasy I'd concocted in my brain became reality, and I'd never felt so cherished and protected.

Falling into complacency came easy, especially once learning from Charley that JD no longer was staying at the motel down near Renovo. Where he'd gone, we didn't know, and I got so caught up in my new life with Charley and Kane, I almost didn't care.

Kane and I remained basically quarantined, and I found I didn't miss my early morning jogs. God knew, the two men gave me a good work out once or twice a day.

On Saturday, Kane headed to Annette and Roy's to finish up the final cabin, and I decided we needed to stock up Charley's cabinets. He agreed to go grocery shopping with me, and I sat behind the wheel of my car for the first time in almost a week, a smile on my face, the carefree sense in my spirit addicting enough, Charley smiled along with me, our hands clasped on my thigh.

An overcast sky hung clouds low in the sky but couldn't diminish my happiness. Two orders had come in through Kane's website—a couple of end tables for his parents and a bed frame for one of his cousins, but still. A sense of satisfaction at helping him begin his own life over added to the layers of happiness inside me.

Charley tucked me against his side while strolling into BI-LO, and warmth flooded through me. Sandalwood and soap … the man smelled downright deliciously wicked.

Keeping my eyes off him as we went through the motions of getting groceries proved impossible. Every wink my way when caught staring rushed arousal to the apex of my thighs. It was as though I *had* found an addiction. I got my fill of their bodies, morning and night, but I couldn't get enough of *them*. Charley and Kane created an insatiable hunger deep inside me, an all-consuming thirst for their laughter, their touch, their attention.

The scent of incoming rain hung heavy in the air, so we scurried to the car with our loaded cart, quiet thunder rolling in along with a gust of wind.

"Hurry!" I squealed, laughing as the first raindrop hit my face.

Every brush of his fingers against mine while loading the bags into the trunk caught my breath—and didn't go unnoticed.

"You're looking at me like I'm a juicy steak, little lady," Charley murmured against my ear as I handed over the last bag for him to stow in my trunk. "I like it."

The smile in his rumbled voice shivered goosebumps over my body, and the squeeze of his palm on my hip spread fire through my insides. I might have gulped. My heart fluttered as I tightened my hold on my keys in my hand.

Another gust of wind whipped my hair across my face.

"Whore."

My head jerked toward my right as my fluttering heart seized over the low tone I recognized from my nightmares.

JD.

"Fucking *whore*! I knew it, you faithless piece of shit!" JD spat, stalking toward us, his shoulders hunched as though enraged and ready to tackle me, his glacial blue eyes taking in Charley's tightening grasp on my hip.

My feet froze, and I stumbled as Charley tried to maneuver me behind his hulking body.

"Get your hands off my wife," JD growled, his last two strides bringing him in with swinging fists.

Charley released his hold on my arm and squared up to meet the rushing asshole, and I fell onto my ass, my keys skittering a few feet away.

JD's fist landed first, but Charley's hit him low, doubling over my ex, the sound of flesh meeting flesh heaving my stomach.

Run. Run. Run.

"D-don't," I gasped out, getting onto my hands and knees, too shaky to stand, reaching for my keys. "Don't hurt Charley..."

Fists and grunts from the two men drew attention, and a woman grasped my arm, helping me to stand. "Are you okay?"

"Stop!" I shrieked at the men, pulling from the woman, and stumbling toward Charley, my chest ice cold. He landed a fist to JD's jaw, knocking him to the ground.

The sky cracked open, spitting cold rain on us.

I grasped Charley's arm, tugging him back, the keys in my other hand digging into my palm as I quickly scanned his face to make sure he was okay.

"Let's just go. Please." My skin crawled, and my stomach roiled. I needed to get out of there—away from JD, away from the stares the fight had drawn.

"Should I call the cops?" the woman asked from behind me.

"No." Charley sniped the word and pulled away from me to stand over JD, who blinked up at the sky. My arms slammed back around my midsection, and I hunkered over, ready to vomit. "She's not your wife. She's your ex, and if you ever come near her again, I'll make sure you spend the rest of your days regretting it."

JD wisely kept his mouth shut at Charley's hissed threat. I shot out an arm to tug on Charley again, my itching feet and racing heart needing us to get away.

"Please, Charley," I whispered, my throat tight and tears stinging my eyes.

He turned and nodded, his dark eyes furious, his face deadpan.

Shaking like the leaves on the trees, I hurried to the driver door as lightning split the sky in half.

Charley grasped my arm, pulling me up short. "Give me the keys." A shadow passed over his face, the glint in his eyes lessening as though pain swept through him.

Heart pounding, I glanced at JD, who had pushed up to his knees, his glare cutting me through the rain.

Run. Run. Run.

I grasped my door handle and jerked it open, but Charley's hand on my arm tightened.

"Give. Me. The. Keys."

Did I trust him to get me away? *Run!* My body decided for me, instinct climbing me through the door and across the console toward the passenger seat, smashing my shin on the steering wheel in the process.

"Hurry, Charley, oh God, please hurry," I whispered, my voice shaking and my pulse throbbing throughout my entire body.

Charley climbed in behind me, and I handed over the keys as I righted myself on my seat. He jerked the driver seat back to make room for his legs and grabbed the keys from my shaking hand.

Rain swept over the car as he backed out, and I turned to find JD standing in the rain, fists at his sides.

"Go," I gasped out, wanting nothing more than to curl into a ball and sink into oblivion, where JD couldn't reach me.

CHARLEY

*R*aging storm. Hurting woman. Driving in the rain.

I refused to make the same mistake twice, and thank fuck, Jill handed over her damn keys, or I'd have torn them from her white-knuckled grip and tossed her ass into the back of her car. Rain slashed at the windshield as I tore out of BI-LO's lot, and I grit my teeth against the rushing memories of Alana arguing with me as the skies poured down over us.

Adrenaline continued to pump through my body, and the beginnings of an ache spread over my cheek from that asshole's first punch. He'd landed a couple others to my body, but nothing I couldn't handle.

Jill curled in the passenger seat, knees to chest, face pale and wet from the rain and her tears. Lips parted, she panted, her eyes wide and glazed over.

"Jill."

She glanced at me, the wildness in her unfocused gaze hitting me harder than JD had managed with his fists.

The fucker hurt my woman without even touching her...

"Seatbelt."

Teeth clenched, I turned my gaze back on the road, fighting for calm as she fumbled to buckle herself in. I should have smashed my boot into JD's face until nothing but mush ground beneath my heel. Better yet, I should have called the cops and had his ass arrested, getting him thrown in the local jail for assault and battery. I knew a few of the guards personally. Had a childhood friend in the slammer who owed me one from our teenage years.

I could have made his life a living hell—better than the death he deserved.

Thunder boomed, and Jill flinched.

"Kane," she whispered, and my thoughts instantly sprang to him, worry twisting my guts.

I opened my mouth to tell her to call him, but an SUV drew alongside us on the two-lane road, the engine roaring.

Fucking JD.

I sped up, an oncoming car in the other lane slowing him to pull behind us again.

Jill whimpered beside me, chanting a muttered *no* under her breath.

"I'm not going to let him touch you," I vowed, thankful as fuck I'd refused to let her drive. We'd have ended up in a ditch or wrapped around a tree for sure with how trembling wracked her body in my periphery.

I sped up, deciding to lead JD straight to the police station, slowing enough to head north on a winding back-road I knew like the lines of my hand. Jill's little car climbed the mountain through the rain, and I kept an eye on JD's headlights behind us, right on our goddamn tail.

Maybe I'd get lucky, and he'd lose control to fly over the

damn guard rails into the trees below. If not, in ten minutes we'd be at the station.

"Call Kane," I told Jill, my tone level, though hell ran riot inside my entire body.

At the first turn, I ignored the yellow arrow sign, hardly slowing, knowing exactly when to turn and how. The car fishtailed in the rain, but I compensated, straightening out without letting off the gas.

The fucker stayed glued to our ass.

"Kane…" Jill's voice broke as she spoke into her cell. "He found me. No. He's following us."

I could barely make out Kane's voice. "Put him on speaker," I barked, glancing in the rearview again.

Lightning and thunder pounded across the sky as one, snaking through the darkness on our right, lighting the valley below.

"Where are you?" Kane asked, his voice tight and small through the cell's speaker.

"Jumper's Ridge."

"What the fuck, Charley?"

"I'm leading him to the station—if I can't lose his ass first."

He stayed close—too close.

Kane swore again. "You're fucking insane!"

I eyed the bend ahead and the gravel turnoff for Sunday drivers' viewing pleasure. That cliff had claimed more than one car in my lifetime.

Sending up a prayer to the God I'd turned my back on, I stepped on the gas instead of letting off like any sane man would do, the thrill of racing like my teenage ass used to do along the mountain road, slamming my heart in my chest— reckless, desperate.

"Charley!" Kane hollered, but I bit my tongue as the rear end of the car slid.

The second JD's SUV hit the gravel and spun out of control, I let off the gas, watching him catch air before disappearing—straight the fuck down.

Relief hit me for half a second before I lost control, the back end of Jill's car sliding too fucking far...

She screamed, and I cursed myself for being a fool.

KANE

The impending storm had sent me packing from finishing the Edwards' cabin to my workshop, the beginnings of fear and nausea less than usual since I had Charley and Jill to focus on. It all came back with a rush at her call.

"Charley!" I hollered again when he didn't answer, Jill's second scream muffled as though she'd dropped the phone.

Rain bit at my face as I sprinted toward my truck, and the sound of crunching metal and sudden silence over the line seized my heart.

"No! Oh, fuck, no. No!" I slammed my door behind me, my shaking hand barely able to shove the damn key in the ignition. Lightning lit the sky, and I cringed, the boom of thunder two seconds later, twisting my goddamn stomach tight into an inescapable knot.

My truck skid and slid on the dirt driveway as I tore down the mountain, and I couldn't calm my racing heart or the pain radiating across my chest as I fought for breath. Adrenaline kept my lungs moving, even as anxiety tried to shut the fucking things down. I didn't even check both ways before swerving onto the main road. Three minutes away … three too many.

Tension rode my entire body, stringing me tight, and I had to mentally pry my hand from the steering wheel to grab my cell off the passenger seat. My fingers shook too fucking much to dial 911, and cursing, I threw my cell back.

Fuck, fuck, fuck.

Another flash, another flinch, more roiling nausea in my gut.

My hands went clammy on the steering wheel as I raced south.

Flashing memories of Alana's car and all the heartache slammed into me with the weight of a fucking freight train. I swallowed against the tightness in my throat, damn tears welling and hindering my view out the windshield as much as the pounding rain and flicking wipers, fighting to do their job.

Pleadings tumbled through my head, a few escaping my mouth as I took a left and raced up the mountain toward Jumper's Ridge. Another cutoff landed me less than a mile from where Charley had said they were, and I stomped on the gas, desperate and scared as hell to reach the top.

I'd given him what I'd fought to ignore for years. Gave Jill what was left of my heart. Allowing myself to love again...

Swallowing back a sob, I drove through the rain, fear over losing them both like I'd lost Alana and Nat crippling my mind. Not many dared the road leading to Jumper's Ridge in full daylight, and especially not during a storm.

Jill's scream.

Crunching metal.

Silence.

Every locked muscle in my body let loose with a shudder, and I took my foot off the gas as I neared the ridge. The guard rail along the pulloff laid torn in half, a gaping hole at its center.

"No … oh, fuck."

I managed to stop my truck and slammed it into park, fumbling with the handle to let me out into the rain.

"Charley! Jill!" I screamed into the wind, racing on shaking legs toward the edge. My heart pounded in my chest, and breaths bursting in and out of my lungs.

I peered over the edge—a mangled pile of black metal and tires lit far below as lightning flashed overhead—no sign of Jill's blue car. Jerking around, I scanned the road in both directions, rain slashing at my face, the wind howling in my ears.

"Charley! Jill!" I screamed and turned in circles, my crippling emotions gaining control over my body.

Help me, Alana. Fucking God, help me...

A sob ripped from my gasping lungs, tears pouring down my face, my legs stilling to face me northward.

Go.

I blinked, my racing mind slowing, my ears ringing, shutting off the sounds of the rain pounding the pebbled ground beneath me. Thunder rumbled but muffled as though I swam beneath eight feet of water.

There.

The bend to my right beckoned—or was Alana's voice whispering in my mind?

Sudden energy sprang my legs forward without thought, and the muffled silence faded, reality crashing back into my ears with the next crack of thunder. My feet slapped the road, my arms pumping in time with my heart.

I rounded the bend.

Jill's car sat down in the opposite ditch, the roof crunched in as though it had rolled, flames licking at the back end. Unable to voice their names screaming in my head, I slid down the bank, my gaze flitting from the flames to the shattered driver's window.

Just like Alana, blood poured down Charley's face—but he didn't blink at me or smile like she'd done.

Stomach heaving, I threw myself at his bent door.

Eyes closed, he sat unmoving other than the pulse thumping in his neck.

Unconscious ... alive.

Jill sat, staring out the windshield.

"Jill!" My holler caused a shiver to ripple over her. No blood that I could see. "Can you get out?" I yanked on the driver's door, but it wouldn't budge. "Fuck! Jill!" I climbed around the car and pulled her door open. The second I grasped her arm, she jerked away, her eyes wide and blinking, unfocused on my face. "It's me, baby. Kane." I managed to lower my voice. "I need to get you out of here, okay? You're alright ... you're going to be okay."

"Kane?" she whispered.

I leaned in and unhooked her belt, glancing over at Charley. A nasty gash lined his forehead, and he still hadn't moved.

"Come on, baby." I pulled Jill's limp body into mine, dragging her from the car.

An engine sounded from the road above us as I dragged

her far from the flames. A car door slammed, but I couldn't be bothered to look up.

"Stay right here. Don't move," I told Jill, my voice fucking unhinged. "I have to get Charley out."

"Are you okay?" a woman called from above, but I didn't have time to answer for Jill.

My stomach heaved as I raced back toward the car, and I swallowed down the bile.

The fucking steering wheel pressed against Charley's chest, but not in a crushing death grip like Alana's had done to her. I climbed in through the passenger door, unhooking his seatbelt.

"Talk to me, Charley, come on, man."

He groaned, his eyelashes fluttering.

"Fucking Jumper's Ridge. What the fuck were you thinking?" I muttered, yanking on the goddamn seatbelt to get it out from under his arm. "I got you. Come on." I yanked and tugged, his groan twisting my insides up tight. "Got you, Charley. Never letting you go."

The second his feet cleared the car, a sob tore loose from me. I dragged him by his armpits back toward Jill, losing my footing twice and stumbling, slamming his body atop mine. Rain continued to pour, sizzling the fire down to nothing.

I settled on the ground beside Jill, Charley in my arms.

The woman had a cell phone to her ear and hunkered on the other side of Jill, her free hand on her upper arm. Jill stared at the car, arms wrapped around her knees.

Reaching out, I wrapped my arm around her waist and tugged until she released her hold on herself and curled up against my side.

Eyes closing, I tilted my head toward the sky and held my

lovers close as the rain washed my tears away, the thunder fading in the distance.

It's going to be okay. They're okay.

"Ambulance and cops are on their way," the woman murmured, and I breathed my thanks to the voice in the wind—whether Alana's or not. Taking her direction toward her brother and Jill as her blessing of us being together, I vowed to myself, I would care for both of them until I breathed my last.

The thought of loss, the fear of losing both had made me realize one thing for certain. I loved them—dearly, desperately. Allowing vulnerability, it seemed, turned out to be worth the risk.

Charley lay in a hospital bed with a few broken ribs and concussion. They kept him overnight, and both Kane and I refused to leave his side, except when the cops showed up to question us about what happened.

JD's car still hadn't been retrieved, but his body had—dead. Good fucking riddance, but I didn't mention that thought out loud. I couldn't find an ounce of regret over the man's death. Hell, I couldn't even find a hair of empathy toward his family, who had always sided with him and looked down their noses at me.

Someone had caught the parking lot fight on video and posted it on social media of all things, which made for an easy self-defense stance for Charley. JD's death had been an accident, plain and simple. There would be no charges. The detective promised to be in touch if need be and left us alone to find what sleep we could in the uncomfortable chairs pulled close to Charley's bed.

Bleary-eyed and aching, we headed back to Charley's in

Kane's truck the next morning. I sat in the extended cab's back seat, my gaze flitting between the two men as Charley told Kane what happened, from BI-Lo until my car slid on the wet road, tumbling us down into the ditch. I'd been lucky to escape with minor cuts and bruises.

Thankfulness for life, thankfulness to be forever free of JD should have had me floating high as a kite, but watching the two men converse, the looks of love they shared, as though I didn't exist behind them, swelled my throat, stinging my eyes with tears.

I was free. Free to go, free to leave them alone, so they could have the life I believed fate had intended. While I found a measure of comfort knowing I'd helped to make that happen, the idea of being without them shredded my heart into tatters, easily blown by the fickle winds of change.

JD's words lingered beyond the grave, reminding me I wasn't worthy of such men. I wasn't a cute, petite blonde. I hadn't been good enough for one asshole man, what made me think I could make things work with two exceptional ones?

Kane helped Charley into the house, and I hung back, my heart breaking even as my body longed for them.

Charley groaned, settling back on the bed, and Kane slid his unlaced boots off his feet.

"Going to tuck me in and kiss me goodnight?" he asked, his tone light and dark eyes twinkling up at Kane.

"Fuck, yes." Kane laughed as though they shared a private joke

I chewed the inside of my lip, my arms finding their way around my middle as I shifted.

Charley's gaze flitted beyond Kane to land on me. His gaze narrowed, and I gulped. "Don't get any ideas, little lady."

Kane jerked around, the light fading from his eyes as well when he saw me hugging myself, ready to sink into the floor and disappear. "Come here." A simple touch to my elbow melted me, and I went willingly into his arms. He smelled like hand sanitizer and musky male in need of a shower, but I sucked that shit down into my lungs, the comfort of his arms easing my anxiety.

"Both of you get your asses over here," Charley commanded, his tone hard. "Now."

Kane chuckled and kissed the top of my head, and we did as told, curling against Charley's sides, although I did so more hesitantly than Kane.

"You're worthy, you hear me? Even if I'm not all that and don't deserve the two of you, I'm a greedy bastard and *want* you," Charley muttered, his hand squeezing my thigh and pulling my leg over his. "Yes, I'm all about this man with us, but I want you, too. I thought I'd made that clear."

Tears clogged my throat and hazed my sight of the two men's heads close together. Dark eyes and hazel eyes, neither of which shuttered what lay inside them, peered at me. The stoic facade Charley hid behind had ripped away, leaving him open, willing, and vulnerable.

Kane's soft smile melted my heart. "You're strong and beautiful," he murmured, and a tear slid down my cheek. "You're everything soft and sweet, Charley isn't."

"Fucker," Charley mumbled, although his lips twitched with a grin.

"I need you, Jill." Kane held my gaze as my heart broke

anew, yet soared through the exhaustion, causing my rolling emotions and insecurities.

Is this what it means to rise from the ashes?

"Say something, Jill. You're killing me, here."

I swiped the wetness from my eyes, my smile trembling. "No one has ever made me feel accepted like you both do."

Kane reached over to brush my hair off my cheek as Charley tugged me closer.

"Stay with us," Kane said, his eyes pleading as though I held the fate of his heart in my hands.

"Please," Charley added.

If falling in love with two men made me a whore in the world's eyes, then I would accept that title—willingly. They made me feel adored. Cherished and appreciated. What more could a woman ask for?

"I'll stay," I whispered, so tired, I didn't want to think anymore.

"You make me so damn happy, Jill." Kane leaned over Charley and brushed his lips over mine. "I never thought I'd find this feeling again."

Both our lips went for Charley's at the same time, and we shared an awkward three-way kiss that ended in light laughter.

Charley let out a sigh and closed his eyes. "Fucking heaven on earth right here."

Kane stared at his face. "You need to rest. I'm taking Jill to shower, then we'll be back."

"Give me something to listen to," Charley said with a smirk even though his eyes remained closed. "Make her come all over your dick, Kane. And, Jill? I want to hear *my* name on your lips when he does."

Drugged up, battered to hell, the man could still bring a rush of arousal straight to my core, regardless of my wanting to curl into a ball and sleep for two days straight.

Kane whispered something in Charley's ear, then held out his hand. "Shower?"

I stank of fear and dried sweat, my clothes dried from the rain the day before stiff and scratchy on my skin. He undressed me with gentle hands, every brush of his knuckles shivering my skin. Exhaustion tugged on my muscles and bones, wanting to sink me into the ground, but his touches, the soft brushes of his lips across my breasts, belly, and pubis while stripping me down, roused my body, soaking me between my thighs.

"Too damn quiet in there!" Charley called out, and I giggled, losing myself in the lightness of Kane's eyes.

Happiness filled his face, the overflow of emotion—*could it be love*—weakened my knees.

He held me beneath the spray in the shower, pulling me tight against his hard body. Forehead pressed to mine, he closed his eyes. "Thought I'd lost you, Jill."

"You drove through the storm for us."

"I'd do it fifty times over, too."

"I'm proud of you." I kissed his mouth, loving the tickle of his water-soaked beard against my skin. "You're one of the strongest men I know."

He pulled back. "Storms always killed me inside, but yesterday, it gave me life—two of them."

"Do you feel like you took back your own?"

Kane considered my words, his hands running up and down my back. "Started on that path, yeah. I think I did."

A smile split my face even as tears welled again. "I've fallen so damn hard for you, it hurts."

His smirk pulsed my pussy with need. So. Damn. Beautiful. "And Charley?" he asked.

"Lordy." A shudder rippled over my skin at the thought of his dark gaze and sure touch. "Yes."

"Come here." Kane pulled me into his arms, pressing my back against the shower wall. His hot breath fanned my face as he shifted to press his hard cock deep inside me.

I gasped, tipping my head back and swallowing the rush of need welling inside me.

"I've got a job to do," he murmured against my ear and nipped at my lobe while sliding out and thrusting back into me.

"God," I groaned, and he thrust again, his arms a tight band under my ass.

"Let me hear your voice, baby. Give him what he wants."

I might have let out my moans and gasps louder than necessary. I cried out Charley's name as Kane took me over the edge along with him, the heat of his erupting inside me, dizzying my brain and wrecking my body.

We found Charley stroking himself when we exited the bathroom a short time later and descended on him, our mouths taking turns with his shaft and balls. His groans had me ready for another round, and when he begged me to sit on him, I climbed aboard willingly—albeit gently.

Slow rocks of my hips took Charley to the edge of release, and Kane captured his mouth and his grunts as he emptied inside me. I collapsed against Charley's other side, unable to open my eyes or make a sound as Kane cleaned between my thighs. He settled against my back, cocooning me between the two men.

Overwhelming contentment and comfort lay like a blanket over my mind—my heart.

Fucking heaven, Charley had said.

So right.

CHARLEY

I made the right choice.

I reminded myself of that when I gingerly stepped into the shower the next morning, even though the decision could have cost Jill's life as it'd done Alana's and little Nat's. My heart didn't believe my thoughts and sat heavy in my chest. Yes, things had turned out okay, but awareness of being unable to keep loved ones safe ate at my mind. I was a lawman and failed those closest to me, almost responsible for another life lost.

Vivid dreams had reminded me of that fact and woke me with the sun.

Jill had still slept peacefully, but Kane stirred and blinked at me with sexy-as-hell green eyes, helping me to crawl from the bed.

Jaw clenched, I took my time washing my body of the leftover blood and sweat, the sponge bath in the hospital hadn't been able to clean completely. Regardless of what I saw as failure, Kane and Jill didn't seem to notice or care. I didn't take well to insecurity. Didn't know how to handle the roiling emotions inside me other than to shut down.

Blowing a heavy exhale through my lips, I closed my eyes and tipped my head back into the hot spray. The shower door clicked open, but I stayed put, the scent of Kane filling my nose and telling me which of my lovers had joined me.

My dick swelled as he ran his hands over the bruising along my torso. Soothing hands, gentle yet needy as they dropped to my hard length that couldn't get enough of him, even though I was bruised to hell and hurting.

Kane moved in, gently pressing his body against mine, rubbing our dicks together. "Jill's making coffee."

I groaned, eyes still clenched tight as my insides warred over shutting down and vulnerability.

"Were you serious about building that addition on my cabin?" Kane murmured, the unsure question in his rasped voice jerking my eyelids open. He peered at me with those sleepy eyes, the vulnerability *he* showed, making me fall in love with him all over again.

I wrapped my arms around him and held him tight, ignoring my aching ribs. "I love you, Kane Austin. Always have, always will. I want you forever. We'd be a couple of grumpy old farts trying to shoot pool long after our eyesight goes if I could have things my way."

The light in his eyes twitched my dick in his grasp, and he rubbed against me. "Sounds like a good plan to me."

"Yeah?" I thrust against him.

"Yeah."

Our mouths came together in a heated kiss, all hunger, teeth, and need, and even the pain rippling across my ribs couldn't keep me from devouring everything Kane offered—his heart, his body, his damn soul.

They belonged to me.

"Tell me you love me, Kane." I bit his lower lip, pulling a groan from his chest.

"I've always loved you, too."

We came together, our bodies entwined, mouths fused, and our dicks pulsing with release against one another.

"I thought I'd lost you when I killed Alana," I whispered, one last shudder running over my skin.

"You didn't kill her." Kane pulled his face away from mine and stared hard at me. "Don't ever fucking say that again. She made her choice."

"Can't help but feel responsible."

"It wasn't your fault."

My throat worked.

"It wasn't your fault," he whispered again.

"I wanted you so damn badly..." I swallowed. "Sometimes, I feel like it's my covetousness that prompted fate to take her from us."

"The fuck, Charley?" Kane's gaze hardened. "Don't you fucking say that shit. I've played all the what-ifs in my head, and all it brought was unrest. It was a goddamn accident. It was their time. Don't you dare blame yourself for what you had no control over."

The confidence in his tone and his eyes, weaseled its way through my thoughts, trying to root itself in my heart.

"Wasn't your fault." Kane kissed my mouth. "Wasn't your fault." He kissed my stubbled chin. "You hear me?"

"Yeah."

"Believe me?"

Fuck, the confidence in his gaze... I lost myself in his love, his acceptance, a well of happiness rising up inside me. "Yeah."

"You spout that shit again, I'll kick your fine ass."

Cocking an eyebrow, I straightened and looked down my nose at him. "That a threat?"

"It's a promise." His sudden grin twitched my lips. "Now, about Jill."

"What about her?"

"You in love with her, too?"

I considered my feelings toward her as I'd done since first catching sight of her at Jenny's Place. Words couldn't describe the connection I'd felt, the need inside urging me to protect and shelter her both physically and emotionally.

"Well on my way," I decided to say, although my feelings for her mirrored those I had for Kane. Would that hurt him, knowing a woman I'd met a few weeks prior, claimed a part of my heart the same as he did with all of our shared past?

"Well, if you want a future with me, then you'd best get caught up," Kane said, grabbing the soap and stepping back like a little brat. "We're a two-for-one deal. She owns that piece of me I hadn't realized I still had to give, and I'm not giving her up—not even for you."

"Gave it over that easily, huh, boy?" I bit back my grin, wondering how the hell two people could entangle my emotions and send them flying fucking everywhere inside my head.

He scowled. "Don't fucking call me that."

I grabbed him and pressed his chest against the back of the tiled shower wall, out of the spray, crowding against him. He caved to my dominance with a groan, his eyes closing.

Biting his shoulder, I watched his lips part, his tongue flitting over the fuller bottom one.

"Boy," I whispered against his ear. Rather than argue, he groaned as I reached around to grip his semi. "Who does this belong to?"

"You," he gasped out as I squeezed. "And Jill," he added quickly as though I needed a reminder.

"And this?" I grabbed his ass with my other hand.

"Yours."

"Mine." I bit his neck, his lobe. "To touch, to tease, to fuck. But..." He arched his back as my fingertips slid down through his crack. A deep groan rumbled clear through his back into my chest. "I'll share this with Jill, too, if she wants it." Water wasn't much of a lube, but I pressed a finger inside him anyway, his hiss jerking my dick.

"Hurt?" I murmured against his ear.

"Don't stop."

"Didn't plan on it, boy."

His growl turned into a whimper as I wiggled my finger in deeper to rub along his prostate. Dick jerking in my hand, he thrust, tightening his ass around my finger.

"Fuck my hand, Kane."

Fuck, did he ever. I ended up with two fingers buried to the knuckle before he came in my hand, his curses and grunts making me hard as fucking nails. Using his cum, I lubed myself up and pushed into his tight heat, my fingers digging into his hips as he leaned forward, shifting to arch his back.

A whimper outside the shower stall drew my attention. The wavering image of Jill stood in the bathroom doorway, and I pulled out and shoved back in with a grin while leaning over Kane's back.

"Our little lady is watching."

Kane's head hung low between his arms, a shudder rippling through him.

I stood and plowed into him again before reaching over to push open the shower's glass door.

Red rose to Jill's face, and she jerked her hand out of her panties.

"Stay," I rushed to say, sure her feet wanted to sprint her away from embarrassment. "Watch me fuck our boy."

"Oh, lordy," she whispered, her gaze dropping to my dick as I pulled out to the head.

"Touch yourself, Jill. Make yourself come."

Lower lip between her teeth, she obeyed, and I fucked myself into oblivion, my gaze on her face, her heaving chest, her rubbing hand as Kane's hot ass squeezed my dick.

"Fuck," I groaned and buried deep, the first shot of cum a goddamn tidal wave of release so sweet, my legs went weak.

Jill cried out, her body curling in on itself, and I imagined shooting the rest of my load alongside her thrusting fingers, drawing out both our climaxes.

"Get over here," I growled at her the second I finished.

She shed her shirt and panties without hesitation, and the three of us stood in the shower together, silent and satiated, until the water ran cold.

"Do it." I stared hard at Jill as she chewed on her lower lip, her focus on Charley, who knelt in front of her. "Say yes."

Tears slid down her cheeks as she glanced at me, ignoring his proposal. "I told you I wouldn't choose one of you over the other."

"And taking his last name is what he and I both want," I argued what we'd discussed a dozen times before, shifting the little bundle in my right arm to the left.

Our son had his father's dark eyes and was just as bossy, the little turd. He squawked and squirmed in his navy-blue onesie.

"See?" I said. "Even he thinks it's a good idea."

Jill laughed through her tears.

"My knees, Jill," Charley grumbled from his kneeling position even though he grinned. "Take the goddamn ring, take my last name, and have the assurance of being taken care of the rest of your life if something happens to me."

"He's got a great pension," I reminded her. "Life insurance, stocks, and bonds."

"Money doesn't mean anything to me," Jill said. "Why can't you accept that taking a ring and saying I do makes me feel like I'm setting one of you aside?"

"You really think I'm going anywhere?" I asked, one of my eyebrows arching.

She glanced at our son.

"Just because it's Woodhill blood running through his veins, doesn't mean he's any less mine," I said, my voice stern.

Charley stood, the open ring box still in his left hand. Fishing in his pocket with his left, he pulled out another, tossing it to me.

I caught the black box one-handed, my brow furrowed. "What's this?"

"Open it."

Flicking it open with my thumb, I stared.

"Can't legally marry you both, but I want you to wear my ring, too," Charley said, his voice soft.

My damn throat tightened.

Charley smiled at me with a lopsided grin—more unsure of himself than I'd seen in nearly two years.

"Seriously?"

"Yeah. Everyone around here knows we're together, so why the fuck not? I've always wanted a ring on your hand, and within a week of meeting our little lady, I knew I wanted one on hers, too. Your parents know my intent. I didn't exactly get the blessing I'd gone for, but that won't stop me from claiming you both as mine for the rest of my goddamn life."

I stood from the rocking chair in our cabin's massive living room and moved in close to my two lovers, enough our son's wiggling toes brushed Charley's arm. Thunder rumbled through the picture window, looking out over our land, and the first raindrops splattered against the glass.

Storms no longer crawled under my skin and filled me with anxiety. Lightning and the sky erupting with deep groans of its own, simply reminded me life's storms didn't always bring heartache. They sometimes brought healing, joy, and eventually, laughter over memories that no longer stung.

"Yes," I told Charley, my gaze unwavering from his face.

He leaned in and kissed me hard above the bundle squirming in my arms.

Jill let out a sigh and snuggled in close. "You two..."

We turned our mouths on her, the sweet scent of her stirring my blood as easily as Kane's kisses did.

"Say yes," I urged, my mouth against her ear.

"Make this greedy bastard a happy man," Charley added.

"I love you both so damn much, it hurts."

I pulled back at Jill's whisper to find tears welling in her eyes again. "I want this for you," I told her. "For us. Make it official. Make us a family. Just because my name isn't on a goddamn piece of paper next to yours, doesn't mean I'm not a part of it." I lifted the ring box Charley had tossed me and wiggled it back and forth under her nose. "See?"

She laughed through her tears. "Fine."

Charley slid the ring on her finger, lifted her in his arms, and claimed her mouth.

I would never grow tired of watching them together. Snuggling my face into the warm little face of the munchkin in the crook of my arm, I smiled, tears choking off my throat.

I'd been given more than a second chance at love. I'd been gifted a second chance at life—with three people I couldn't imagine being without.

Alana hadn't spoken to me since the day I pulled her brother and Jill from the car, but she'd led me to them. I didn't doubt *her* blessing, the only one I needed.

I also didn't doubt the meaning behind our son's grimace.

Oh, shit!

An explosion sounded in his diaper, and I held him away from my body … too fucking late.

"How's that working for you?" Charley asked with a laugh while I eyed the mustard-like stain on my shirt.

"It isn't, asshole," I grumbled the obvious truth. "Your son shit on me."

"*Our* son."

"Yeah." I smirked. "I'll take care of this mess, then put him down." I eyed my lovers, who still stood in one another's arms, recognizing the look of lust in both their eyes. "Don't you two start celebrating your engagement without me."

"Hold up." Charley grabbed the box from my free hand, retrieved the band, and slid it over my ring finger. "Ready to grow old with me?" he asked quietly, the love in his eyes making me forget all about the stench and stain on my shirt.

"Been ready."

"Good." Charley brushed his lips over mine. "Now go change him and put him in his crib. *We've* got a mess to make."

I hurried off, Jill's carefree laughter overshadowing the sounds of the storm outside. With Charley, Jill, and our son,

I'd found peace, true contentment. I wouldn't change my past, given the opportunity. Yes, life shit on the three of us at times, but it also led to where we were truly meant to be—wrapped in love so sweet, the storms no longer brought a fear of loss.

THE END

ABOUT THE AUTHOR

Lynn Burke is an international bestselling and award-winning author. A stay-at-home mom, she's a lover of coffee and vino, and with three spawn and two fur babies underfoot, noise levels dictate the daily switch-over time. In her few quiet 'me' moments, she can be found hunched over her Mac, trying to type as fast as her muse spews hot stories.

You can find more about Lynn at her website: www.authorlynnburke.com